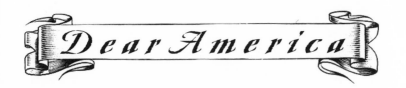

Hear My Sorrow

The Diary of Angela Denoto, a Shirtwaist Worker

BY DEBORAH HOPKINSON

Scholastic Inc.   New York

New York City
1909

Tuesday, September 14, 1909

Today I stayed behind to tell Miss Kelly my news. I stood quietly by her desk while she corrected papers, waiting for her to notice me. All I wanted to do was blurt out what I had to say and run home.

Miss Kelly is the prettiest teacher at school. Her skin is creamy, not olive like mine, and she has freckles sprinkled on her nose, like cinnamon. Usually her eyes are light blue. But suddenly I noticed they look stormy and dark, like the seas we crossed to come here from Sicily. I felt a knot in my stomach, for it almost seemed as if Miss Kelly was angry with me. But what had I done?

Miss Kelly tossed her pencil onto her desk, heaved a heavy sigh, and turned to me. "I already know what you have to say, Angela," she said. "I've heard it before. You've just turned fourteen, and you're leaving school."

I let out my breath. "*Sì*, Miss Kelly. My father commands me to work in a shirtwaist factory."

I'd hoped she would be proud of me. After all, I would be helping my family. But, instead, she frowned and pulled at the tucks of her own crisp, white shirtwaist blouse. Then she opened her desk drawer.

"Some Jewish girls stay in school until they are fifteen, even sixteen. Why must these Italian parents send their children to work at fourteen? And this one is so bright . . . ," Miss Kelly murmured to herself, almost as if I weren't standing right there, or couldn't understand English.

But I did understand. After all, I am no *grignolla* — no greenhorn — who has just arrived in America. I've lived in New York City for four years now.

My face flushed hot, the way it always does when I'm embarrassed. I stared down at my shoes, which used to be Luisa's. Now they're almost worn out, especially in the heels. I wanted to explain, to tell her more. But I lifted my chin and pressed my lips together. Our family has pride.

"I suppose your parents won't let you go out at night to attend evening school, either," Miss Kelly went on, sighing again. "Ah, here it is. Angela, this is for you."

Then she put this book into my hands. For the first time, she smiled. She told me it was a gift because I am quick and bright, like a sparrow. She said she hated to see me leave, because I am smart enough to finish eighth grade, and even become a shopgirl someday, if I want. I felt my face get hot.

Miss Kelly said she hoped I would keep up my English,

even though I wouldn't be coming to school anymore. "If you bring this diary back filled, I'll give you another," she promised.

Fill a whole book! At that, my mouth dropped open. I couldn't think of what to say, so I just mumbled, "Thank you," and walked away. I didn't look back.

As my shoes clomped across the wooden floor, I heard her grumbling to herself, "I'm not sure why I bother. How many diaries have I given away? No girl has ever brought one back."

Later

If Miss Kelly had been here yesterday afternoon, when *mio padre* came home clutching his shoulder, his eyes bright with pain, then maybe she'd understand better why I have to leave school.

As soon he walked in, Mama had jumped up and cried, "Pietro, you're hurt!"

"Nothing, it's nothing." He sank into the chair and bit hard on his lip as Mama helped him off with his jacket. She moved gently, as if he were little Teresa sick with one of her breathing attacks, instead of a strong man, the head of the household.

I wish my papa didn't have to work so hard as a hod

carrier. Those loads of bricks on his shoulders are heavy. The hod is like a big tray, and the boss makes him pile it high and move quickly to bring bricks to the bricklayer. No wonder his old hurt keeps returning.

I knew Mama needed to finish her order of artificial flowers for ladies' hats, so I stayed at the kitchen table, putting yellow centers into blue forget-me-nots. Mama brought strong coffee, just the way Babbo likes it. He settled back and watched me, rubbing his shoulder. After a bit he spoke to Mama, using the words of our village back in Sicily. "Angela is a smart girl, no?"

Mama shrugged and refilled his cup. "She is fourteen now. Old enough to work."

I felt Mama's dark eyes on me. Just last week I'd gotten up the courage to ask if I could stay in school another year, to finish eighth grade. Mama had promised to think about it. But now I brushed those thoughts aside. I knew what my duty was.

I took a breath. "I'm ready to go to work, Babbo. And Mama, I . . . I don't even like school anymore."

Babbo raised one eyebrow, then nodded. Mama smiled, satisfied. Ducking my head, I bent to my work. It felt good to please my parents.

This is the right thing to do. I like school a lot, and I'm good at it. But school is a world Mama doesn't under-

6

stand. I never really expected her to allow me to finish eighth grade, even if Babbo hadn't gotten hurt again.

Later, when Luisa came home, she told me how to get working papers from the Board of Health. Luisa says she can get me a place as a learner at her *scioppa*, the shop where she works as a sewing machine operator.

Well, that's that! Soon I'll be a factory girl. I'm glad I'll be able to help, especially now that Babbo is out of work. Yes, helping my family is what's most important.

Still, tonight as I write, I can't help thinking about Miss Kelly. I keep remembering her eyes, daring me to fill these empty white pages. She probably thinks I'll be like those other girls who never brought their diaries back. Well, maybe I'll show her that I'm different.

Wednesday, September 15, 1909

This morning I got my working papers. Later I went to the market for Mama. Mama says I'll make a good wife someday because I can add numbers in my head and never get cheated. Still, she always gives me strict instructions. I must buy from *paesani* — friends, relatives, and neighbors from the western part of Sicily, like us.

"Anyone else is a stranger — not to be trusted," Mama warns.

So I always go to the Caccioppos' store for "loose" milk for six cents a quart, except when Teresa is sick, when we buy clean milk in a bottle for eight cents. We get olive oil from the Riggios, because they live upstairs, on the third floor of our tenement building. And Mama has her favorite fish, cheese, and fruit vendors, too.

Today she reminded me to buy bread from the Cavellos' bakery. "Go there last, Angela, so the bread doesn't get crushed in your basket like last time."

Teresa came along, and Mama's voice followed us as we made our way down the dingy hallway. "Now pay attention, Teresa. When Angela's a factory girl, I'll need you to go to the market sometimes by yourself if I'm too busy."

"*Sì*, Mama," Teresa called back. But as soon as our feet hit Elizabeth Street, she grabbed my hand and held on tight. She's only eight, and doesn't like the crowds.

The pushcart vendors shouted in our ears, urging us to buy from carts stacked high with glistening fruits and vegetables. People were everywhere — pushing, talking, yelling. Children darted in and out.

I saw one boy bump a bright-red apple off a cart. Before I could blink, his little brother had swept the apple up off the ground and sprinted away before the peddler could hit him. The peddler threw his fist in the air and started to yell, making his face turn as purple as an egg-plant! Teresa and I had to turn away to hide our giggles.

I love the market now. But I can understand why Teresa feels shy. When we first came here I was only ten, and each time I stepped off our tenement landing I felt sure someone would knock me down! Our village in Sicily was noisy, that's true. But not like this, with people scurrying everywhere, like ants and no trees or grass in sight.

Teresa was only four when we left, so she doesn't remember much. But I do. Back home our stone house had a loft and two rooms with dirt floors. Beyond the edge of town I could look out at neat rows of grapes and patches of golden wheat. Mama grew flowers in front and in the small *cortile*, the courtyard we shared with our neighbors.

It didn't seem to matter so much that our house was small, because we spent so much time in the *cortile*. That's where Mama and the other women did their household chores, and where Mama taught Luisa and me to wash clothes, sew, and make macaroni. The *cortile* made it easy for mothers to keep watch over their little ones. Here, though, mothers are always shouting down at their children from the high tenement windows.

Still, as Mama always reminds us, life was harder back home. Every day, since she was as old as I am now, she had to walk to the town well to fetch water. Mama wouldn't give up having a cold water faucet right in her own kitchen for anything. And even though our village was pretty, times had gotten so bad *mio padre* couldn't get work, even as a farm laborer.

After we'd gathered everything Mama needed at the market, we went to the bakery. Arturo gave me a big smile as we walked in. He's only fifteen, but his *padre* depends on him a lot in their business. We waited while he helped an elderly woman, then he said, "My sister Tina says you're not at school anymore, Angela. Is that right?"

Tina was in Miss Kelly's class, too. I told Arturo my plans. Arturo is easy to talk to, unlike most boys. His eyes are so friendly and warm. Today he even gave us an extra loaf of day-old bread for free. And when we left, he called out a cheery *"Ciao!"*, even though he was already busy with another customer.

On the way home, Teresa pulled on my sleeve and teased, "He certainly smiles at you a lot. Is he your *boifrendo?*"

I shook my head and pinched her arm. "Teresa, you're becoming too American! Mama will help find us husbands someday, you know that. Besides, Arturo smiles at everyone."

But later, as I ate Arturo's bread, I couldn't help smiling myself.

Before Bed

Luisa got home from the factory late tonight. She was so tired, she barely touched her macaroni before her head started to nod. Her food didn't go to waste, though. Vito grabbed her plate and ate the rest. At thirteen, he's growing so fast, he can eat a mountain of macaroni every day!

Soon I'll be working long hours, too. I'm a little worried about not being here for Teresa. She depends on me a lot. I like to do the shopping for Mama, but Teresa would rather stay home. I help Teresa with her schoolwork, too. And that will be hard to do if I get home late.

Sometimes I worry, too, because Teresa doesn't seem very strong. She sleeps right next to me, and wheezes a lot at night. I guess the dust and dirt of our neighborhood don't agree with her.

Saturday, September 18, 1909

Luisa brought home bad news, and Mama's not happy about it. The new orders for shirtwaists have been delayed, so I can't start work on Monday, and will have to wait a few more days.

I hope the boss doesn't change his mind. What would we do then? Mama is good at managing our money, but with Babbo not working, she's already worried about coming up with fourteen dollars to pay next month's rent.

Mama kept me busy all day, scrubbing the kitchen floor and helping her cook soup. But now I have a little time, so I'm sitting on the fire escape as I write. It's dirty and dusty, and the noisy crowds are just below on the street. Still, at least I *feel* alone here.

I'm never alone in our apartment. Sometimes I think Mama has brought our whole village with her to New York City! *Paesani* bang in and out of our door from morning till night. Our whole tenement building is noisy, bursting with laughter, shouting, crying babies, and pounding footsteps. To make it worse, our apartment is right in the middle of things, in front on the second floor, and everyone comes to Mama for advice — and for her strong, rich coffee — the best in the building.

We have "aunties" and "uncles" everywhere!

Luisa seems to fit right in. Maybe it's because Luisa and Vito take after Mama. They like to talk, laugh, tease, and gossip about everything under the sun. Teresa is quieter, like Babbo. As for me, well, I guess I'm in between.

It's not that I'm quiet, exactly. Luisa would say I ask too many questions — and that I'm too serious. I know one thing: I definitely don't like being the center of attention, with everyone's eyes on me. That's why I hid this diary under my arm just now. I just know Zi' Maria, our neighbor on this floor, would click her tongue if she saw it.

I can hear her now: "Writing in a book, what nonsense! American schools make trouble between parents and children. It's better that Angela goes to work to help the family. It won't be long before she'll be married, anyway. What girl needs writing and English? She should do her part now."

And then I can imagine Zi' Rosalia, a wiry older woman who's always bragging about her granddaughter, chiming in: "Tsk, tsk! We had no nonsense like that with Giuseppa. She's only sixteen, and, like Luisa, has been a fine, working girl, bringing good money to her mama every week. Soon she will be married. . . ."

Even Luisa shook her head when I showed her Miss Kelly's gift. When I start work at the factory, she told me, I won't have time for such foolishness. She teased, "Just tear out the pages now, and use them in the toilet!"

That made me mad, but Luisa's probably right. She thinks she is, anyway. Ever since she turned sixteen it seems like she scolds me almost as much as Mama does. We used to be close, but lately I've noticed that something's changed. For one thing, she spends all her free time with Rosa, whose family lives above us.

Not long ago, I overheard Babbo telling Zi' Vincenzo,

Rosa's papa, how well I could read English. Even though I wasn't the one bragging, Luisa narrowed her dark eyes and flashed me an ugly look.

Sometimes I wonder if Luisa is just a little envious. Maybe, after all, she wishes she could have gone to an American school like me. Luisa had to go to work as soon as we arrived in New York, even though she was only twelve. That made it harder for her to learn English — not that she needs to speak it in our neighborhood. Maybe once we're working together, Luisa and I will get closer again, the way we used to be. I hope she'll talk to me more, instead of only to Rosa.

Oh, here's a sparrow. He's a bold fellow — he's landed so close to my feet. I love how he hops about on the iron landing and cocks his head at me. He's probably searching for one last meal before dark. I wish I had some crumbs to give him. I wonder if Miss Kelly is right: Maybe I *am* like a curious sparrow.

Well, there I go, thinking about Miss Kelly and school again. Zi' Maria may be partly right. School hasn't exactly caused trouble between my family and me, but I think in a way it *has* made me a little different. More American, maybe.

It's safe to tell the truth here in this little book since I'm the only one here who can read English in my family. And so I can write that when I told Mama I didn't like school, well, that wasn't exactly true. I did like school — a lot. But as Mama and Zi' Maria say, why should a girl go to school when her family needs her help, and she will soon be married, anyway?

No, here in America, work is the most important thing. As Zi' Maria would say with a laugh, "Here, it is *worka worka* all the time."

Tuesday, September 21, 1909

No news about my job yet. Luisa says the *bosso*, Mr. Klein, is waiting for new orders to come and the busy season to start. Every day that goes by, Mama gets more anxious, since our rent will soon be due. I wish I could start my job so I could help out.

I can't help wondering what the factory will be like. At first I thought I'd have to sew a whole shirtwaist blouse all by myself. Back home, being a *sarta*, a seamstress with scissors dangling from one's waist, is an honored profession. But Luisa says it's different here. It takes about ten workers to make one shirtwaist. Some girls sew just the collars or the seams of the sleeves. But Luisa says I won't even be sewing at first. I'll be a learner, snipping off the ends of threads.

Tonight I asked Luisa to tell me about the girls in her shop. She explained that besides Italian girls, there are many Russian Jewish girls who speak Yiddish. There are even some American girls and a few Irish girls.

"Usually the boss puts girls who speak different languages next to one another, so they won't chatter," Luisa said. "And it's just as well. There are some girls who would make trouble in our shop."

I wanted to ask Luisa what she meant by "trouble," but just then Mama asked her to take some soup upstairs to Zi' Caterina, Rosa's mama, who hasn't been well.

As for me, I think I'd like to make friends with a Jewish or an American girl. I can think of so many questions to ask. I'd like to know what their families are like, where they came from, and what they eat. I know Jewish people usually eat different foods than we do. Teresa and I sometimes go to the Jewish market on Hester Street, where there's lots of meat, huge pretzels sprinkled with salt, and strong-smelling pickles swimming in barrels of brine.

Friday, September 24, 1909

Flowers, flowers, flowers! My fingers are sore from making artificial flowers for ladies' hats. We've been working on them all week, because as soon as Mama heard I couldn't start work at the factory, she didn't waste any time. She went right to Mr. Silvio and got an extra-large order of artificial flowers so we can earn our rent money.

Mama usually brings Teresa with her when she goes to get flowers, because Mr. Silvio has his favorites. He pinches Teresa's cheeks and teases her, which Teresa doesn't like at all.

Today, while my fingers were busy, I couldn't help figuring in my head how much money we'll make. In a way it's a little like the number problems Miss Kelly gave us.

We get paid ten cents for each gross — 144 flowers — we make. Sometimes Zi' Maria works with Mama. And so does Rosa's mama, Zi' Caterina, when her little boys, Alfio and Pietro, are at school. But I don't think Zi' Caterina has worked for several weeks now. By herself, Mama can make enough flowers to earn about sixty cents a day. On days when Teresa and I help, we can make twelve gross — more than 1,700 flowers — a dollar and twenty cents.

Last night Babbo said he would try to get work next week, but Mama won't hear of it yet. She says his shoulder must heal more.

"Ah, how you take care of all of us, Mama," he teased her.

At Bedtime

We had so many flowers to finish tonight! Even Vito, who'd rather be running in the streets with his friends, pulled up a chair at the kitchen table. We do almost everything in our kitchen, especially in the winter, when we want to be near the warmth of the stove. This little room is our *soggiorno*, our main living and eating area, and at night it's Vito's bedroom, too.

Babbo doesn't usually help with flowers, although Teresa tells me that the other afternoon when she came home from school she found him working along with Mama at the table. Most evenings, though, Babbo goes to his favorite café on Mulberry Street to talk and play cards with Zi' Vincenzo and other men from the neighborhood.

"Is it roses, violets, or daisies?" Vito asked.

Mama smiled. She pampers Vito, and never scolds him as sharply as she does us girls. "Violets, for spring hats."

Teresa picked apart petals while I separated stems. I dipped each end into paste spread on a board on the table. Mama and Luisa slipped the petals up the stems. Vito tried to help, but his fingers aren't as quick as ours are. His tongue makes up for it, though. Before long he was boasting about how much money he'll make when he starts work.

"You should work in a candy factory, Vito," Teresa suggested. Teresa loves candy, especially *torrone*, almond candy, but we don't usually have extra money for such treats.

Luisa smiled and said Vito would hate working in a candy factory. She told us about a girl in her shop named Maria who once worked in one. Maria had to peel coconuts and almonds all day long. The work was dirty and made her hands hurt. Worst of all, she only got four dollars and fifty cents a week.

Vito snorted. "Well, then, I won't work in a candy factory — I'll own one! I heard an Italian started the Margarella Candy Company. You wait! That'll be me someday — a rich businessman."

It's hard not to smile at Vito's bragging. He began telling wild stories of all the fancy things he'll buy in the big department stores uptown once he's rich. Before long Teresa was laughing so hard, she started to wheeze. Mama clucked her tongue and sent Teresa to lie down.

Sunday, September 26, 1909

Yesterday Luisa brought home her pay envelope and gave it to Mama without opening it. Luisa says some girls in her shop keep money back for themselves. Imagine! Why, that's almost like being a boarder. Mama would never allow that, although with Vito it might be different. Boys have more freedom, after all.

Usually Mama is pleased with Luisa when she opens the envelope, but this time she snapped, "Luisa, there are only six dollars here. Last week you brought home seven."

Luisa hurried to explain. "*Sì*, Mama, but remember, the cloth for the new shirtwaists didn't come on time, so one whole morning we sat in the shop, just waiting. They didn't pay us for that time. And don't forget, Mama, there are the costs."

Luisa has told us about the costs. She has to pay twenty-five cents each week for a locker to keep her hat and coat in. She also has to buy her own sewing needles, at five cents each. If she's late, she pays a fine. Still, Luisa feels lucky to have this job. Sometimes, in the slack season, when the work slows down, many girls lose their jobs. Then when it's busy, they work long hours, without overtime pay, in a frenzy to keep up. That's just the way it is, Luisa says.

Mama frowned. She does that a lot lately. She has two little lines on her forehead that don't go away. She asked Luisa again if there would be work for me.

Well, I've saved the biggest news for last: Luisa told us the cloth and new designs have finally arrived. That means the busy season is starting and the boss says it is okay for me to come. Tomorrow I become a factory girl.

Monday, September 27, 1909

Luisa shook me when it was still dark. But I'd been lying with my eyes open for a long time, my mind as crowded as Elizabeth Street. Would the boss like me? Would I make friends with the other girls? Would I be able to learn my new job?

Teresa was still asleep next to me on our folding bed in our *salotto*, our good front room. Her dark eyelashes curled on her cheeks like the tiny feathers on my sparrow. I shook her gently. Vito was spread out across the chairs in the kitchen. He's getting so tall, he won't fit there much longer. I could hear Mama making coffee and grumbling at him to wake up. That's not easy — Vito can sleep through just about anything.

Outside, Luisa handed me a roll, but I felt too nervous to swallow even a crumb. I stuffed it in my pocket for later. I clutched my scissors, carefully wrapped in a bit of paper.

Mama had given us ten cents each for the elevated train. But Luisa suggested that we walk instead of taking the El. "It's not that far. Besides, I'm saving for a new hat for next spring."

It wasn't even seven, but the streets were already crowded with people rushing to work. *"Buon giorno, buon giorno."* We said good morning to everyone.

The busy season must be starting everywhere, because we passed several shops advertising for workers, with signs reading, GOOD PAY, LONG SEASON. Luisa had had to leave her first job because in the slack season only the senior machine operators were given work. She was left to sit, day after day, not getting paid. That's when Rosa told her about this shop.

When we got there the first thing that happened was. . . .

Tuesday, September 28, 1909

If Miss Kelly ever reads this book, my face will turn red with shame. Last night my eyes closed in the middle of a sentence.

I've washed the dishes in our little sink. Teresa and Vito are doing lessons (although the last time I looked, Vito was dozing off). Mama has gone upstairs to take some nice *zuppa* to Zi' Caterina, who's feeling poorly again. These days, she only has enough energy to eat soup. The gaslight is dim, but I can see well enough to write about my new job.

The shop is on the third floor of an old building. Perhaps thirty or forty girls work there. Luisa says some factories have hundreds of hands. We had to walk up creaky wooden stairs in a dark hall. The stairs were grimy and I wanted to hold my nose, the smell was so bad.

Luisa led me past an outer room with large tables where a few Jewish men were already at work. The men using the heavy irons were pressers, she told me. Others worked as cutters, bent over large wooden tables and laying out thin paper patterns to cut sleeves or collars using short, sharp knives.

We stepped into a large room where girls were just sitting down to their machines. There are two long tables, and I counted about ten or twelve sewing machines on each side. Even though there are some windows on one wall, the room is lit mostly by gaslight. The floor is littered with snippets of thread, remnants of cloth, dust, and lint. The dust tickled my nose and I sneezed.

Luisa pushed me to stand in front of Mr. Klein, a bony man with dark hair and smudged glasses on his nose. The boss peered at me. "So, are you the new cleaner, the trimmer? Do you speak English?"

"Yes, sir, I went to school for four years."

"Humph," he grunted.

Suddenly, a bell rang and the machines sprang to life. A whir filled the air. I could feel the wooden floorboards under my feet quiver from the vibrations. Needles flashed and jumped. Up and down, up and down. The electric current was on!

The *operatrici*, the operators, bent to their sewing machines. The girls looked so determined as they guided the cloth under the fast needles. At the end of the rows, other girls sat trimming threads and stitching collars and cuffs.

Mr. Klein turned to snap in Yiddish to a girl who was coming in. I would have been scared, but she simply looked at him calmly.

"Go with Sarah," he told me, pointing at her. "Since she's late, she can lose even more time from her work to teach you. And remember, in this shop there's no talking. Ten cents' fine if you talk."

I was too scared to ask if I could sit near Luisa. But it wouldn't have done much good, anyway. The boss frowned and waved us off.

I followed Sarah. She looks about eighteen or nineteen. She has curly, dark hair, sturdy shoulders, and flashing brown eyes. All her movements are quick, as if she has important things on her mind and no time to waste.

Sarah led me to a table at the end of the row of whirring sewing machines. Luisa sits halfway across the room at the other long table, but Rosa is just a few machines away.

Luisa was busy, her head bent, but Rosa glanced up for

24

a second. She smiled, ever so slightly, her head nodding quickly. Mama says Rosa is named well — she's like a flower that brings smiles to people's faces. I think Mama is right. Looking at Rosa made me feel better, as if she knew my hands were shaking. I had to clasp them together to keep them still.

"You'll sit here, near me, at the end of this row," Sarah told me. Then she ordered, "Stick out your hands."

I put my hands out, hoping she wouldn't notice them trembling. She peered at them closely. "All right. Be sure they are clean. Always. If they're dirty, you'll soil the cloth and ruin the waist. Understand?"

I nodded.

Sarah pointed to a pile of shirtwaists. "This is your stint, your pile of work. Now, do you have scissors?"

I nodded and pulled out my scissors.

She grabbed them. "A cleaner's job is to trim the threads off the finished shirtwaists. Look, cut like this." She began to snip threads from the sleeve of the shirtwaist so fast that the blades of the scissors flashed. "Go as quickly as you can. Be careful not to let your hand slip. Now do it while I watch."

Sarah stood beside me while I snipped the loose ends of the white threads from the insides of the sleeves, first one sleeve, then the other.

"All right, but faster. Remember, clean hands. And fast."

And so I began.

By the time lunch came, my stomach was making little growling noises. I wanted to go outside and walk in the air. Many of the girls sat by their machines to eat. A few whispered quietly. Others left to use the toilet or walk in the hall. Anyway, lunch was only a half hour. I took my roll out of my pocket and nibbled it slowly to make it last.

And then it was back to work. Snip! Snip! Snip!

The scissors made my fingers red and sore. I wanted to shake my hand and rub the hurt away. But I didn't dare stop for an instant. No one stopped. Every girl in the room was sewing as fast as she could. Whenever I wanted to stretch, Mr. Klein was peering over my shoulder.

Once he barked, "Don't stop, girl."

The afternoon dragged on. Then, from somewhere outside, I heard bells chime six. I felt sure we would stop then, but no one moved. I couldn't wait to stand up and stretch. Oh, how I wanted to go home. The minutes dragged on. Six, six-thirty, seven.

Just when I couldn't stand it a minute longer, the machines fell silent. It was seven-thirty. My eyes were blurry and my back ached. I followed Luisa and Rosa home, hardly knowing where I was walking. We said nothing. I felt a dull pain in my head. My fingers were cramped and sore.

We climbed the dark stairs and said good night to Rosa. I asked Luisa if there would be overtime pay. She shook her head and told me we were paid by the week, not by how many hours we worked.

Then she said softly, "You'll get used to it."

Friday, October 1, 1909

It's been just a few days, but I already know my job well. It doesn't take half my brain to snip threads all day. It's not nearly as hard as the number problems Miss Kelly used to give us. But it makes me tired and sore. If only the chair I sit in had a back.

Today in the middle of the morning I felt a sharp pain creeping up my spine. I wanted to move and stretch to make it go away, but I was afraid to stop working. Mr. Klein had his sharp eyes on me again. So I kept my head down. Snip! Snip!

Mr. Klein let us go a little earlier today. When I got home, Mama sent me to the market with Teresa. As we came down the steps, Teresa squeezed my hand and whispered, "I missed you. I'm glad you're with me, Angela."

We darted quickly around carts selling dried fish, bananas, tomatoes, and long strings of garlic and shiny, red peppers. There's so much beautiful food — and such wonderful smells. Garlic, cheese, coffee, and fresh bread. Teresa and I love to stand in the pasta shop and crane our heads back to look at strings of noodles hanging down like ribbons.

Mama needed bread. As we entered the bakery, Teresa poked me in the ribs and whispered, "Arturo's here, Angela."

Arturo flashed a smile, as if he really was glad to see me. "How's your new job?"

I shrugged. "I'd much rather work in a bakery," I said. "It smells nicer here."

"You wouldn't like getting up before the birds," Arturo teased.

I had only a nickel, for a day-old loaf of bread, but Arturo gave us a fresh eight-cent loaf, anyway. I like the bakery, with the crusty, rich loaves piled on wooden trays. Why, there's even bread on the walls, hanging like wreaths.

"Please take good care of my little sister whenever she comes here," I asked Arturo as we left. He smiled and promised he would.

Arturo seems to like working in his father's bakery. If our papa had his own small shop instead of being a hod carrier, everyone in our family could work together. I wouldn't care what kind of business it was: a butcher shop, a small grocery, or maybe even a confection shop. Vito and Teresa would like that!

Yes, if we had a business of our own, I wouldn't have to work for a boss who scowls all day long. I think Mr. Klein has a heart like a raisin.

As we passed by the small barbershop on the corner, Teresa pulled on my sleeve. "Look, there's Babbo."

Teresa was right. There he was, sitting inside with a group of men. But he didn't see us. He was bent forward, listening closely to a young man whose hands were moving wildly as he talked.

Babbo seemed so interested. Of course, it wouldn't be proper for a girl to question her father. But I couldn't help wondering what they were talking about. And who was that young man?

Saturday, October 2, 1909

The end of my first week! Tonight we left the shop at five. Her eyes sparking, Rosa linked her arms into Luisa's and mine. "Let's celebrate your first week of work, Angela."

Rosa pulled us into a shop and bought us pieces of almond candy with pennies she'd saved. She gave me two pieces, but I saved one for Teresa. Oh, was she pleased!

Mama was happy, too. I felt so proud as I gave her my first pay envelope. I don't make as much as Luisa, but at least I'm doing my part.

Sunday, October 3, 1909

My day off. I helped Mama clean the apartment and now I'm back in my own special place — the fire escape. It's fun to look down at the crowds rushing by. I hope my sparrow will visit, since I remembered to bring some crumbs to feed him.

I feel so tired. Yesterday as we rushed out of the shop, I heard a girl named Clara sing softly, "I would rather sleep than eat." Even though I've only worked one week, I can understand this song. Some nights my whole body has ached so much, I didn't care about eating. And in the morning it begins all over again.

At least Babbo's shoulder is better. Tomorrow he'll go see his friend, Mr. Rizzo, who works as a mason. Mr. Rizzo often helps him find work. Maybe he'll get a job soon.

I wonder if Babbo once dreamed of having a lot of money, the way Vito does. He doesn't talk about such things anymore, but I know he still thinks we're better off here in America.

Just last evening, as I served coffee to Babbo and Zi' Vincenzo in the kitchen, I heard them talking about how bad things are in Sicily, and how hard the workers and farm laborers have been fighting for change.

Miss Kelly always talked to us about the importance of reading. Mama and Babbo may not be able to read, but they still seem to know about everything that goes on — even back in Sicily. It's almost as if our neighborhood itself is a newspaper.

Tuesday, October 5, 1909

This morning, Clara Ruben, the girl I heard singing the other day, had an accident on her machine. The sewing needle went right through her finger and pierced her bone. Clara turned white as the cloth under my hand. She put her head down. I thought for sure she would faint.

Mr. Klein did nothing. "Go back to work," he growled.

I kept cutting threads, but I couldn't keep my eyes still. Already I've gotten good at watching everything around me and still doing my work. Of course, whenever Mr. Klein turns my way, I pull my eyes away fast. Luisa's warned me never to draw attention to myself.

Suddenly I sensed a movement near me. It was Sarah

Goldstein, the girl who showed me how to cut threads on my first day. Sarah stood up and walked over to Clara.

I was shocked. What would happen next? Would Sarah get fired for leaving her machine?

Sarah bent over Clara, then straightened up. I could see beads of sweat on Clara's forehead. She looked like she might be sick. Sarah said something in Yiddish to Mr. Klein. He frowned and began to yell, waving his arms.

Sarah ignored him and helped Clara out of her chair. She happened to look my way and our eyes met, just for an instant. Then they walked out, with Sarah supporting Clara. Straight out the door. I could hardly believe it.

"Go back to work. What are you looking at?" Mr. Klein growled. Quickly I ducked my head. Snip! Snip!

I couldn't wait for the bell to ring at the end of the day so I could talk to Rosa and Luisa about it. As we walked home I asked, "Why was Mr. Klein so mean? Wasn't he worried about Clara?"

Luisa turned to me with a fierce expression. She said this had nothing to do with us. "Don't get involved, Angela," she warned. "Those Russian Jewish girls like to make trouble, especially that Sarah Goldstein. Stay away from her."

I stammered, "But, Luisa . . . she only wanted to help."

Luisa gave me a dark look. She was about to say more when Rosa came between us and took each of our arms.

"Come, my friends," she said. "I have a few pennies for candy today."

But even the sweet candy did not make the bad taste of the day go away.

Wednesday, October 6, 1909

I couldn't help looking around as I walked to my table this morning. I didn't see Clara anywhere. When Sarah came in, our eyes met. I started to open my mouth to ask her a question, but even from across the room I could sense Luisa's disapproval.

When the bell rang for lunch, Sarah got up from her chair and looked my way. I stood up and our eyes met again. I followed her into the hallway. I couldn't control my curiosity any longer.

"Is that girl, Clara, all right?" I whispered.

"Her finger will be fine. But Clara isn't strong. She's only nineteen, and already she's worn down with work," Sarah answered in a low voice. She shook her head. "What Clara really needs is a good, long rest. But she'll be here to-morrow. Clara needs this job — she's the only support her mother has."

"Oh," I breathed. I didn't know what else to say. Would that happen to me in five years, I wondered? Would I already be worn down?

"That's why we have to work for better conditions," Sarah went on in a whisper. "Do you know about the union?"

But even before I could answer, Sarah was telling me about the union she'd joined, Local 25 of the International Ladies' Garment Workers' Union, the ILGWU. She said the time had come to fight for our rights, and she hoped something might happen this fall.

When the lunch break was over, I sat down, picked up my scissors, and began to snip threads as usual. Snip snip, snip snip. But with every snip my thoughts flew. What did Sarah mean: Something might happen?

Later

Tonight as we sat at the table, helping Mama make flowers, I told Luisa what Sarah had said about Clara's health, and how her mother needed her so much. I thought that would make her change her mind about Sarah. After all, Sarah had just been trying to help her friend.

"I think it was a brave thing to do," I said softly, when Mama had gone upstairs to visit Zi' Caterina for a while. But Luisa only shrugged and pressed her lips together.

34

Luisa is so hardheaded. She's decided that Sarah Gold-stein likes to make trouble, and that's that. Nothing I say will make her change her mind.

Friday, October 8, 1909

Oh, how I wanted to stay snuggled in bed this morning. But I pulled on my clothes and followed Luisa down the dark, smelly stairway, barely opening my eyes. I trudged past a scrawny cat curled in a tight ball under a box. I felt so tired, I wanted to lie down beside him.

Luisa was cross with me all the way to the shop. She's still mad because yesterday at lunch I stayed in my chair and chatted with Clara and Sarah instead of eating with Rosa and her. I guess because she's my older sister she likes to be in charge of me.

I told Luisa I was too tired to move, and that talking to Sarah gives me the chance to practice my English. Clara still seemed a little pale, but she didn't complain about her energy. Instead, she wanted to work on her English, too. But of course that's not the only reason I like talking to Sarah — and Luisa knows it. Sarah is like no one else I've ever met. She seems to burst with ideas and energy the way Elizabeth Street bursts with people.

Just yesterday, when Clara said she was having trouble

learning to read English, Sarah told us how she'd learned to read novels in English.

"Once, soon after we came here, I bought a copy of a novel by a man named Charles Dickens from a pushcart vendor on Hester Street," Sarah said, her eyes glowing. "It was called *Great Expectations*. My English was so poor then, but I made myself finish the whole book. After each page, I wrote down every word I didn't know and looked them up in the dictionary. Then I read the pages again.

"And that's how I did it, page by page. I learned more from reading that book than from school. My favorite part is the beginning, when Pip meets the convict on the dark, empty moor."

Sarah laughed. That's just the way she is. She gets so excited about things, it makes you excited, too. And even though I don't think I'll ever be able to read a long book in English, listening to her makes me want to try.

I would have liked to talk to Sarah again today, but I don't want Luisa to get too angry with me. So I took my roll and ate with Luisa and Rosa. It's a good thing Luisa can't read English or understand this diary — then she would really be mad.

•   •   •

Mama asked me to take some bread to Zi' Caterina tonight. Rosa's mother was lying in bed in the back bedroom, with two neighbors beside her, mending and chatting. I stood in the doorway to give Mama's greetings. Then Alfio and Pietro, who are seven and nine, begged me to stay and help them with their schoolwork. Like Luisa, Rosa hasn't been to school in America, so she seemed glad when I said yes.

"You are so smart. Isn't she?" Rosa beamed.

I blushed. "I like reading and numbers and I help Teresa all the time."

As we sat at their small kitchen table, we could hear Zi' Caterina coughing through the thin walls. Alfio flinched every time his mama coughed.

Suddenly I had an idea. "Rosa, maybe Pietro and Alfio can come down to our flat in the evenings. Then I can help all the children together."

Rosa's eyes strayed to the bedroom. "*Grazie*, Angela," she said softly.

Saturday, October 9, 1909

Today Sarah and I talked for a few minutes during our lunch break. Sarah told me about herself and her family.

She's eighteen and went to school for six years in America. For the last three years, though, she's worked so her younger brother, Joseph, can stay in school.

Sarah's family came to America from Russia about nine years ago. "I was only nine years old when we left, but I remember being afraid. The government had many rules for Jews — where we could live, and what kinds of jobs we could have."

Sarah was silent for a minute. "We lived in a *shtetl*, a village only for Jews," she went on softly. "People were poor, and many families struggled to survive. And then there was a *pogrom*."

"A *pogrom*?" I repeated. The word sounded familiar.

"Soldiers came," Sarah said flatly. "They burned houses. They killed innocent people. My uncle died."

I thought about Sarah's words all afternoon. More than half the girls who work here are Jewish. I wonder what their lives were like before they came to America.

After work, Luisa and Rosa wanted to walk to the park at Washington Square. "Just for a little while. It's Saturday, after all, and tomorrow we're off," said Luisa.

The park was crowded with girls, laughing and talking. The Triangle Waist Company is just one block away, in the tall Asch Building, at the corner of Washington Place and Greene Street.

Outside the Triangle factory, girls with signs were pacing up and down on the sidewalk. I pulled at Luisa's sleeve. "What are they doing?"

"Picketing. The workers there are on strike."

Rosa stopped to look, too. "It's not a strike anymore. I heard Sarah Goldstein, that girl from our shop, say it's a lockout."

"What's a lockout?" I wanted to know.

Rosa wasn't exactly sure, but she thought that, after the girls went on strike, the owners closed the factory. When they opened it again they hired new girls instead of the striking workers. That meant these girls were locked out, and had lost their jobs.

I looked at the girls with their signs. "So they're being punished for going on strike."

Luisa pulled me away, frowning. "They've lost their jobs. You see what happens, Angela, when you talk to girls like Sarah."

I was just about to answer when a young man with a thin, strong face came up and greeted Rosa. Luisa smiled, then grabbed my hand and pulled me back behind them as we walked along.

My mouth fell open. It's not proper to walk and talk with strange men on the streets. Surely Luisa and Rosa know that.

Luisa whispered his name: Audenzio Maniscalco. "If you'd get your head out of your little book, Angela, you'd realize you've seen Audenzio before. His father has the barbershop on the corner, where Babbo often goes to meet his friends. Audenzio isn't a barber, though. He works as a cloakmaker, making fine ladies' cloaks."

The barbershop! I looked at him more closely. Yes, he was the same young man Teresa and I had seen Babbo talking with so earnestly. The one with the wild, moving hands.

Just then Audenzio turned around and caught me looking at him. He gave a quick nod, but he didn't smile. His eyes were bright and sharp, a little like Sarah's.

In a low voice, Luisa told me that Audenzio's mother is a distant cousin of Zi' Caterina, so their families have known each other for a long time. I should have realized Rosa would never get a boyfriend on her own. She would never violate the *onore di famiglia*, the family honor. Luisa told me that Rosa's parents, Zi' Caterina and Zi' Vincenzo, approve of Audenzio. She feels sure Audenzio and Rosa will become engaged someday, but this isn't a good time, while Zi' Caterina is so sick.

Later

As usual, our kitchen is full of friends and neighbors, including Zi' Maria. As I slipped out to the fire escape, I made sure to hide this diary in my skirts.

My sparrow flew right up next to me just now. He hops about and cocks his head at me. Soon he will fly off. I wonder where he sleeps at night.

Even though it's almost dark, Elizabeth Street is still full of people. I wonder where they're all going. Sarah told me she sometimes attends lectures at the Educational Alliance in the evenings. She's even been to the theater to see a play. It sounds exciting, but I know Mama needs me home at night.

Sunday, October 10, 1909

The toilet in the hall was plugged today, for the second time in a week. Mama and Zi' Maria (naturally!) don't think Mrs. Cassio does a very good job of being the building manager.

"You should be the manager, Mama," said Vito. "You would do a good job. When I own a tenement building, I'll hire you." Mama shook her head at his nonsense. Then she smiled, licked her finger, and tried to pat Vito's hair into place. He laughed and squirmed out of her grasp.

Vito is right, though. Mama *would* be a good manager. Although I don't think it can be easy to take care of a tenement building. So many people moving all the time. When we first moved here, we didn't pay rent for the last month at our old building. Sometimes I think Mama would like to move and do that again. But she won't leave so long as Rosa's family needs us. Besides, so many of our *paesani* live here now.

Tomorrow is Monday — laundry day. Mama will be up by six, to wash clothes in water made boiling hot on our big black stove. Then she'll hang everything out on lines outside the rear window. Before long it'll be cold and rainy or even snowy, and then we'll have to hang the clothes in the kitchen to dry. Doing laundry is one job I don't like! Still, as Mama always says, washing clothes is easier here than having to trudge to the town well for water.

Mama and Zi' Maria will also do laundry for Rosa's family in the morning. Rosa has to work, and Zi' Caterina is too weak these days. Nobody has told me, but I've overheard enough to guess the truth. Zi' Caterina has the disease everyone dreads: tuberculosis.

Thursday, October 14, 1909

Can it be Thursday already? I've been too tired to even open my diary this week. But I just had to write today. I can't stop thinking about what I saw this morning. Right outside our shop there was a man whipping an old work-horse, trying to get her to pull a wagon. The man looked almost as old and tired as the horse. The horse seemed to just give up, and stood with her head hanging down and her sides trembling.

I passed by, hardly stopping to look. Then, out of the corner of my eye, I saw Sarah coming down the street from the other direction. To my surprise, she went up to the man and spoke to him in a low, intense voice.

Luisa grabbed my arm and pulled me up the stairs into the shop. But she can't stop me from thinking about what I saw. Sarah is like no one I've ever met before. She seems on fire inside, and wants to fight all the injustices in the world, starting right here.

"Angela, if we don't speak up for ourselves, who will speak for us?" Sarah said later, at lunch. "We will be like that poor, dumb animal in the street. That is why we must all join the union."

I didn't answer. I'm curious, but I'm not really sure what

to think about all of Sarah's ideas. Besides, Luisa says the union is only for Jewish girls, not us.

Friday, October 15, 1909

Good news. Babbo worked today! Mama was so pleased, she hummed to herself as she made the macaroni tonight. As I worked beside her, taking out plates and forks from the cupboard for our meal, I couldn't help smiling. I liked the sound of her low voice.

"I remember how you sang Teresa to sleep back home, when she was just a baby," I told Mama.

But at that, Mama became quiet and stopped humming. I wondered if she was thinking of her own mother, who died last year. How hard it must have been for Mama to say good-bye to her family and everything she had known, and come to a strange, new place.

At least *mio padre* was able to travel with us. We were lucky that way. Sarah told me her father had come to America more than a year before the rest of her family. He couldn't send for them until he'd earned enough money to pay for their steamship tickets.

"My poor mother! She spoke not a word of English, and she was so sick and frightened during the voyage. She barely let us out of her sight the whole time," Sarah said.

"And when they separated the boys from the women and girls for a physical exam at Ellis Island, she thought she'd never see my brother Joseph ever again!"

Sunday, October 17, 1909

Teresa has a bad cold. Her cough is rough and makes her chest ache. Her wheezing is worse when she has a cold. Sometimes she has a hard time catching her breath.

To help Mama, I went to the market. Arturo was working in the bakery and gave me an extra-large loaf of bread. Arturo is a little like Rosa. He always smiles before he frowns, and that makes me smile, too. But why must my face get so hot and turn red whenever I try to say even a few words to him?

Later I helped Mama cook the macaroni. Then we sat down to make artificial flowers. While we worked, Luisa and I took turns singing to Teresa and telling her stories. Even Vito told one.

At least Vito was home today. He's been gone most afternoons after school lately, Teresa tells me. That little brother of mine had better be careful! I hope he doesn't get in with some of the wild boys who steal from the pushcart vendors. It's one thing to follow coal carts or wagons to find scrap pieces of coal or wood. Everyone does that. But stealing . . . Vito has big ideas, but sometimes I'm afraid he wants to do everything the easy way.

I wish Vito could stay in school longer. But I know as soon as he turns fourteen he'll leave school and go to work.

Tuesday, October 19, 1909

The girl who sat next to Sarah has quit. Suddenly this morning I heard my name. Sarah was speaking up for me with Mr. Klein.

"Give Angela a chance to be a machine operator," she said. "She's a fast worker and a quick learner. Also, her English is good, especially for an Italian girl. She'll help explain things to the other Italian girls and make things easier for you."

She said more, but in Yiddish, so I didn't understand. But as I snipped I held my breath, waiting for Mr. Klein's answer.

Mr. Klein scratched his chin and turned to stare at me. He nodded toward my stint and pushed his smudged glasses back on his nose.

"After you finish, sit there. She will teach you. If you make too many mistakes, you'll have to go back."

It took me until late afternoon to finish the shirtwaists in my stint. Then I sat at the machine next to Sarah and watched. That's when I first got scared. How will I ever make my seams as straight as hers?

"Come a little early tomorrow morning," Sarah offered. "Mr. Klein will be here, getting the cloth ready to be cut for the new styles. He'll let us in, and I can explain it to you better. You won't make so many mistakes, and I won't lose time from work teaching you."

Luisa's mouth turned down even more than usual as we walked home. "I don't like you being near that girl."

I didn't answer. But Luisa was the quiet one when I told Mama that, from now on, I'll be a machine operator, too.

Wednesday, October 20, 1909

Today was my first day as an operator. On the floor to my right stands a wicker basket piled high with my work. As I sat down in the wooden chair, I could smell the oil of the machine.

At first I was so nervous, my hands shook, like on my first day. But Sarah is a good teacher. She spoke clearly and showed me each step.

I'll start with simple seams first. I must lean forward

and run the cloth under the vibrating needle to make each seam. I have to concentrate every second. This job isn't as easy as trimming threads.

At lunch I took out my roll. "Thank you for teaching me and for talking to Mr. Klein for me," I told Sarah. "You could have tried to get the job for a Jewish girl."

Sarah smiled. "Well, you're a good worker. Why shouldn't I help you? I don't like that the bosses always separate Jewish and Italian and American girls. They don't want us to support one another, or talk to one another about what we want to change. I hope we'll all fight together — soon."

Talking to Sarah makes my head whirl. I can never understand half of what she says. What does she mean, "fight together"? I just don't see that there's much hope that things will change.

I keep thinking about the Triangle factory. When the Triangle workers went on strike this fall, there were other girls just waiting, desperate for work, ready to take their jobs. That's just the way it is.

Sometimes I wonder if Luisa is right. Maybe Sarah does want to make trouble. Still, without her, I wouldn't have this new job.

Friday, October 22, 1909

Yesterday I had an accident. Mr. Klein kept telling us to go faster and faster so we could make a deadline. All at once my hand slipped and my finger got in the way. The needle went right through. I felt a sharp, sudden pain.

Oh, it hurt! I wanted to scream. I bit down on my lip hard, trying not to cry. Sarah reached over and handed me a piece of cotton. "Bind it up with this and make sure you have some with you for when it happens again. That way you can keep sewing quickly."

Sarah says these accidents happen to everyone, especially when we're asked to sew fast. Luckily, the needle went through part of my nail, which isn't so bad. When it happened to Clara, the needle went right into her bone. That must have really hurt!

After that I concentrated hard so I wouldn't make mistakes. But, oh, how my back and shoulders ached. Luisa says it will get better once I can relax. But how? I have to pay attention every second and go as fast as I can. Last night when we came home I was so tired, I couldn't write in this book. All I wanted to do was sleep!

Today I sat in my chair and talked to Sarah at lunch. I told her how happy Mama is about my new job. *Mio padre* might make more money, but Mama is the one who keeps the family going.

Then Sarah told me a little about her mother, who still wears a *sheitel*, an old-fashioned black wig, like married Jewish women back in Russia do. Sarah smiled. "We try to make her change, but she's attached to the old ways."

I nodded. I often see Jewish women on the streets with their dark wigs, shawls, thick wool stockings, and big, sturdy shoes. I think our mothers aren't so different. Luisa and I hate to look like foreigners. We wanted to get rid of our foreign clothes as soon as we came to New York. But Mama still wears her old shawl, and doesn't mind if she looks like a foreigner.

"Mothers don't need to worry about getting married, like we do," said Sarah with a sly smile. "At home my mother would sew us new clothes just a few times a year, at holidays. Here in New York I want to look stylish, like an American."

Sarah told me a funny story about her little brother. When her family came to America, Joseph had heavy, clunky old shoes, made by the cobbler back home. He didn't like them at all. "Joseph hated being teased by the other kids," Sarah told me.

But Joseph knew his parents would never agree to buy new shoes until his old ones wore out. Sarah smiled. "One day Joseph came home with only socks on his feet. He'd thrown his shoes in the river so he'd never have to wear them again."

Of course, Joseph was punished. But Sarah's parents had no choice but to buy him a pair of American shoes. I couldn't help laughing.

"Joseph sounds like he's a rascal," I told her. "That's exactly the kind of thing my brother Vito might do. But, oh, would my parents be angry."

Sunday, October 24, 1909

Rosa came to fetch Luisa today, so Luisa could help her at home. Zi' Caterina isn't any better. I can tell Rosa is worried about her mother because she only gave Teresa a small smile when she came in. Mama had made some soup for Rosa's family. Little Alfio looks like Rosa, with his long eyelashes and shy smile. When Vito teases him, he always hides his head behind Rosa's skirt.

Zi' Vincenzo works as a day laborer, taking his pick and shovel wherever he can find work. But the work isn't regular, so the whole family depends on Rosa's pay. It's a good thing Mama, Zi' Maria, and the other women in our building are here to help.

Tuesday, October 26, 1909

A girl who sits near me got sick this morning. She had to use the toilet twice before lunch. On the third time, Mr. Klein followed her into the hallway and began yelling in a loud, scratchy voice, urging her to hurry. I'm lucky I don't get sick easily. Sometimes I try not to use the toilet in the hall for the whole day. But other times I must.

We worked until nearly eight tonight. The order was late, and Mr. Klein pushed us hard to finish. By the end of the day I was so tired, I could hardly see.

But Sarah didn't seem tired — instead, she was angry! As we spilled onto the sidewalk from the factory, Sarah put her hand on my shoulder. She leaned forward and looked right into my face with flashing eyes. "Angela, you've been to school, so I know you can read English. I want you to take this."

She thrust a newspaper into my hands. In big letters on the first page it said *The Call*. Sarah whispered low and earnestly. "Read for yourself why we must do something about the way we're treated!"

I was so surprised, I couldn't say a word. At that moment Luisa grabbed my arm. I tried to push the paper back at Sarah, but she was already rushing away.

I stuffed the newspaper into my pocket and said nothing to Luisa and Rosa about it on the way home. I ate some macaroni and helped Teresa, Alfio, and Pietro with their schoolwork.

But when my chores were done, I took the newspaper into the toilet with me and read some of it, until Zi' Maria began banging on the door, shouting for me to hurry. "I've heard about you and your little book, Angela," she shouted. "I hope you're not writing in there. Other people live here, too!"

I put the newspaper back into my pocket and opened the door. I showed her my empty hands. "I wasn't writing, Zi' Maria," I said. Then, quick as a flash, I slipped past her into our apartment, leaving her shaking her head at me.

Anyway, from the part that I did read, it seems to me that *The Call* is more for Jewish workers, and how they should join a union.

I wonder what Babbo thinks. Sometimes when Zi' Vincenzo and Babbo are sitting and drinking coffee in our kitchen, I've heard them speak of the *fasci dei lavoratori*, workers' unions, that are still active in Sicily. I wonder if Babbo was ever involved in one back home?

And what about Audenzio, Rosa's friend? When Teresa and I saw him in the barbershop, Babbo and several other grown men were all paying close attention. What could such a young man say to make them listen like that? What were they arguing and talking about so intensely?

Thursday, October 28, 1909

Yesterday as we left, Mr. Klein scolded Luisa because she hadn't finished her stint. Luisa is usually a fast worker. Suddenly I realized her skin was glistening with sweat and her eyes looked watery.

Outside, I reached up and put my hand on her forehead. "You have a fever, Luisa!"

She began to cry. All the way home, Rosa and I held her tightly under her elbows, even when people jostled and pushed us. Once, I thought she would faint. At home I pulled out our folding bed, and Luisa rolled into it without a word. Mama clucked her tongue and got a cool washcloth for her head.

Luisa thrashed in her sleep all night, and this morning her skin felt hot. She cried, "I can't be sick. What if I lose my job?"

But she couldn't even sit up, never mind go to work.

This morning the power went out in the factory for a while, so all the machines stopped. Mr. Klein was busy trying to fix the problem. For a few minutes, no one paid any attention to us.

Sarah leaned over and asked what I thought about *The Call*, the newspaper she'd given me. I shrugged, not knowing what to say. Sarah raised her eyebrows. Finally I admitted I didn't really understand much of it.

"Well, you're young, and just starting out. But if you keep your eyes open, you'll see why we must stick together and fight."

Bending close, Sarah told me in a whisper about something that had happened when she'd worked at the Triangle Waist Company.

One of the foremen was a nice man who had hated to drive the girls so hard. "When he tried to protest to the bosses, they fired him," Sarah remembered. "As he left the room, he pleaded, 'Brothers and sisters! Don't let me be treated this way.'"

I looked around to make sure no one was watching us. "What happened then?"

Sarah shrugged. "We walked out for three days, then we came back. The bosses made speeches and promises but, in the end, nothing changed. Angela, the truth is that unless we all join the union and work for better conditions, nothing will change."

"Luisa and Rosa have thought of getting jobs there," I said. "They think it would be nice to work with so many girls, and be so near a park like the one in Washington Square."

Sarah shuddered. "I'd never go back to the Triangle factory! For one thing, it's ten stories tall and you have to work on the eighth or ninth floor. The bosses keep some of the doors locked so no one will sneak out or steal anything."

Sarah talked more about unions, but I didn't understand everything she said. She reminds me of a strong, young horse. Her eyes flash, as though at any minute she might bare her teeth and bite, or rear up and kick. I don't think she could ever be beaten down.

When the power came back on, Mr. Klein yelled at us to work faster to make up for lost time. Sometimes he stands over my shoulder, peering at my work. He is so close, his stale breath touches my ear.

Friday, October 29, 1909

Luisa is still sick. Our rent is due in a few days, and Babbo only worked half of the month. So early this morning Mama and Teresa left to get an order of artificial flowers from Mr. Silvio. Teresa stayed home from school to help.

Somehow, though, no matter how bad things are, Mama always seems to manage. She makes sure our rent is paid and food is on the table. She even does her best to make the apartment look cheerful. We have bright curtains for our windows and a few pictures on the walls — thanks to Mama.

I thought of Mama when the shop peddler came in today, carrying a basket of food. He stopped near me and lifted the black oilcloth from his basket so I could see the bright red apples and sweet rolls tucked inside. I was so hungry. In my pocket I had the dime Mama had given me. I wrapped my fingers around it, longing for a bite of sweet, crunchy apple. But I shook my head. I can get by, and save my money for another day.

Listening to Sarah has made me curious to learn more about the union, so tonight I read *The Call* again. It said that the union wants to help workers fight for the "three eights": eight hours of work, eight hours of free time, and eight hours of sleep.

Sarah says the factories are not supposed to make us work more than ten hours a day, six days a week. And we should have a full hour for lunch, not thirty minutes. All the factory bosses ignore these rules, though.

Well, no matter what Sarah says, I don't think this will change. If we protest, they'll just hire new workers.

Sunday, October 31, 1909

Luisa's a little better, but now Vito and Teresa are sick. Vito thrashes about fiercely and when he's awake, he begs Mama for water. He says his body feels like the train tracks with the El running over him! But Teresa doesn't complain, even though sometimes I hear her gasping for breath.

Mama is beside herself. She has flowers to make, and the apartment needs cleaning. I don't think she'll be able to wash our family's clothes tomorrow, let alone help Zi' Caterina. I worked as fast as I could to make flowers, then helped her cook beans for supper.

Babbo ate in silence. At first I didn't think he liked my cooking, but at the end of the meal he told me the food was good. I jumped up to take his plate and do the dishes. Mama was in the next room, helping Vito get a drink of water.

"So, you are a machine operator now, Angela," Babbo said. "You are a good girl."

His words made me feel proud. It was just the two of us in the kitchen, and more than anything I wanted to ask him what he thought about workers and unions. But if he wants to talk about it, he will bring it up.

Monday, November 1, 1909

I wanted to stay at home and help Mama take care of everyone, but it's the busy season now. Mr. Klein kept us sewing until after eight o'clock. By the end of the day I was so tired, I spoiled a waist. I didn't mean to, but Mr. Klein says it must come off my pay.

Rosa and I rushed home in the dark. A peddler jostled against me, and I stepped into a puddle. I could feel the cold water seep into my shoes.

Poor Rosa! I shouldn't complain — at least Mama is here to take care of us. But I'm afraid Zi' Caterina is getting worse. Every day Rosa rushes home to do chores and take care of her mama. At least we are lucky to have *paesani* here to help out.

Like tonight. When I walked down the hall, Zi' Maria opened her door, pulling Rosa's little brothers after her. She must have been listening for my footsteps. "Ah, there you are, Angela. Alfio and Pietro have more schoolwork to finish. Tonight you must be their 'little mother.' Take them to your kitchen now and help them. I've already fed them some good macaroni. And when they're done, wash their faces and take them to Rosa to put to bed."

"*Sì*, Zi' Maria," I answered, taking little Alfio's hand. I felt tired, but I'd never dream of disobeying Zi' Maria.

Besides, I don't mind taking care of younger children. Even though I'm only a year older than Vito, when we first came to Elizabeth Street, Mama often asked me to be his "little mother" out on the street, keeping watch while he played with his friends. Now, of course, Vito is old enough to fend for himself.

From the grim, tired look on the boys' faces, I think they realize their mama is very ill. But they won't be neglected, not while Zi' Maria lives in this tenement. I don't always like Zi' Maria's sharp eyes, but if she sees something that needs doing, she makes sure it gets done. Zi' Maria and Mama look out for everyone.

Thursday, November 4, 1909

Luisa and Vito are better. But Teresa is so weak this morning I had to help her get to the bathroom in the hall. Zi' Maria was in there, and so we had to wait, which made me ten minutes late to work. I'll be fined for that. It doesn't matter how long we work at night — if we're even a few minutes late in the morning, we get fined. If I'd tried to explain, Mr. Klein would just say, "If you don't like it, you know what you can do."

Sarah and Clara say all factories are this way. Today, Clara told us about the factory where she used to work where she made ladies' corsets. "I had to pay thirty cents for each spool of thread I used, usually two or three a week."

Sarah's eyes flashed. "That's just what I mean. You probably earned less than six dollars a week, working long hours. So why should you have to pay for your own thread?"

Sarah went on to say that the problem is that most of the bosses, like Mr. Klein, are subcontractors. Mr. Klein is our boss, but he doesn't own this factory. He gets orders from a bigger boss. That's why Mr. Klein tries to pass off all the costs he can, like thread and needles, to the workers. That way, he can make more money.

"No matter how you look at it, the workers lose," Sarah told us.

From talking to Sarah, I am getting to know Clara Rosen, too. The other day at lunch Clara asked me for help with her English language lesson. She's taking a class from the Women's Trade Union League, the WTUL, a group of American women who volunteer to help working girls. Sarah explained that the WTUL is like a partner to Local 25 of the ILGWU.

As I looked at Clara's lesson I was surprised. It wasn't like the lessons we had in public school. It was all about the problems of workers like us — how we work overtime without pay, and how we must pay for our own needles and thread.

After I helped Clara with some of the harder words, I couldn't help myself — I kept reading. One part described a girl who worked in a union shop:

> *She goes home at twelve o'clock on Saturday.*
> *She has one hour for lunch every day.*
> *Sometimes she works overtime in the busy season.*
> *She gets extra pay for overtime.*

Imagine — working only a half day on Saturdays. If this is what the unions want, it's no wonder the bosses are against them.

Still, I can't help thinking how nice it would be. If I had Saturday afternoons off, I could go to the market for Mama, or even take Teresa to special festivals. We could listen to music, watch the parade, and stroll up and down looking at all the carts and booths full of delicious things to eat.

Or maybe I'd just sit on my fire escape, write in my diary, and wait for my sparrow to visit me.

Monday, November 8, 1909

At lunch, Sarah whispered that she had something exciting to tell me about the Women's Trade Union League. She said that most of the WTUL members are well-off American ladies. They've been to college, live in fancy houses, and are married to rich men.

"One morning last week the WTUL president, Mary Dreier, was picketing with girls in front of the Triangle Waist Company," Sarah said, her eyes flashing with excitement. "Mary Dreier begged one girl not to cross the line and be a strikebreaker. Well, what do you think? That girl struck Mary Dreier, then told a policeman to arrest her!"

"Did he do it?" I asked.

Sarah nodded. "Yes, but was that police officer surprised when they got to court and found out that Mary Dreier was a rich American lady. He said he'd never have arrested her if he had known."

Mary Dreier told her story to the newspaper. So now Sarah hopes that the large American newspapers might pay more attention to what's happening at the Triangle factory. Maybe more people will support the girls there, and their right to strike peacefully.

Sarah isn't sure about trusting rich American ladies like

Mary Dreier, but she says the Triangle strikers need all the help they can get.

Tuesday, November 9, 1909

A needle broke on my sewing machine this morning. At first I didn't know what had happened. There was a jerk, a funny noise, and then the thread started spinning around.

It was easy enough to fix. But now Mr. Klein will take off from my pay for the broken needle. As mean as Mr. Klein can be, though, I've learned that ours isn't the worst shop. Sarah says a friend of hers works for the Bijou Waist Company, where the boss moves the hands of the clock when he thinks no one is looking. He gives the girls only twenty minutes for lunch instead of thirty.

Later, as Luisa walked upstairs in front of me I noticed a hole in the bottom of her left heel. No wonder she got sick walking in the wet, cold streets. Shoes cost about two dollars, sometimes more. But Luisa has her heart set on a new hat for spring, and she's saving for that.

As for me, I think I'd like to have an umbrella, for when the rain comes down hard. My hair is so thick that once it gets wet, it seems to stay damp for hours. But an umbrella costs at least a dollar. I'd also like a pair of gloves. I saw some in a pushcart on Elizabeth Street for seventy-nine cents.

Every week I have to pay twenty-five cents for a locker to keep my coat in at the shop. But if I didn't have to pay for broken needles, and had that locker money to keep for myself, I could easily save to buy an umbrella or some gloves.

Tonight Mama grumbled when we arrived cold and wet. She doesn't like this weather, either. The other day I heard her tell Zi' Maria that she misses the sunshine of Italy on these dark, cold days.

"Italy is beautiful but poor," replied Zi' Maria, shaking her head. "Here at least there is enough food, and we can eat until we belch."

Mama smiled and patted the faucet in the kitchen sink. "And I wouldn't trade all the sunshine in Sicily for this."

Thursday, November 11, 1909

It's hard to pick up my little book today. I feel so tired. It's because Zi' Caterina died yesterday. All evening, Rosa's apartment was crowded with *paesani*. Rosa's pretty face was streaming with tears. I took Alfio onto my lap, and Pietro snuggled beside me. I know it's selfish, but I couldn't help thinking about what we would do if something happened to Mama.

All the women in our tenement will help cook and care for Zi' Vincenzo and his family now. After all, they are *paesani*, and whatever we have we will share. Babbo will help Zi' Vincenzo arrange everything. The funeral will cost more than a hundred dollars. Each family will give what it can.

Just before we all went to bed, Luisa dropped some coins into Babbo's hands. "For the funeral," she said. "I've been saving up the dimes Mama gives me."

"That money was for your spring hat," I whispered, once Luisa and I were in bed.

Luisa turned her face away from me and didn't answer.

Monday, November 15, 1909

Rosa was back at work today. What else can she do? Each time I see the dark shadows under her eyes, I feel like crying.

Everyone is sad. Yesterday afternoon Mama stared out the window, trying to wipe away the dirt on the pane, searching for blue sky. She is missing Zi' Caterina and Sicily, too.

Sicily seems so far away, like dreams that fade when I open my eyes. Only feelings and colors are left behind. But here on Elizabeth Street the tall buildings seem to cover up the sun. And now that it's November, the sky is gray and gloomy, like a bitter old man. Babbo says his shoulder hurts, a sign that winter will be long and hard.

Today Vito came home with pieces of coal for our stove, which had fallen off a cart. He took some to Rosa's family, too. He is a sweet boy sometimes.

I hardly sit outside to write anymore. But tonight I took some crumbs from my piece of bread at supper and left them on the fire escape for my sparrow. I wonder if he will make it through the winter ahead.

Wednesday, November 17, 1909

There's always a rush down the stairs when we leave the factory. Last night I got separated from Luisa and Rosa. As I stood waiting for them on the street, I heard two girls talking near me. One was Sarah.

"Workers at the Triangle and Leiserson shops have been fighting alone. But many girls are joining the waistmakers' union, Local 25 of the International Ladies' Garment Workers' Union," Sarah was saying. "Local 25 is small, less than 800 members, I think. But now the union has called a mass meeting for next Monday night."

She lowered her voice. "Something is sure to happen."

My head turned. I couldn't wait to hear what Sarah would say next, but at that moment Luisa came up. With a scowl, she began to walk so quickly, I had to run to catch up. Still, as we hurried along, I couldn't help thinking about the girls who have been striking this fall.

I think they're so brave to walk on a picket line with a sign. I can't imagine doing such a thing. I would feel afraid of what might happen to me. I wouldn't want to be arrested by a big, burly policeman, or have people look at me or taunt me. And what would Mama think? No, it would be so much easier to try to get another job instead.

This morning I felt as if someone had left a window open, and a fresh, new breeze was blowing into our shop. It must be all this talk about change.

Mr. Klein growled to himself, barked orders, and paced back and forth across the factory floor like a nervous watchdog. Next to me, Sarah bent to her machine with her usual concentration. But I could sense her impatience and excitement.

"Something *is* about to happen at last, Angela," Sarah whispered as we slipped into the hall at lunch. "Why, even Samuel Gompers, the president of the American Federation of Labor, will be at the big meeting next Monday night."

Sarah said she hoped they would decide on a general strike. "A general strike? What does that mean?" I asked.

"A strike by everyone, by *all* shirtwaist workers. Not just a shop here and there, the way it has been all fall. Will you come to the meeting, Angela?"

I imagined what it would be like, sitting in a large hall, surrounded by other working girls. But of course I shook my head. My parents expect me to be home at night.

Sarah told me that her father works as a cloakmaker and belongs to a different union, but he has always supported her. From reading *The Call*, it seems like many Jewish men like Sarah's father are involved in unions.

I didn't say anything. Lunch break was over then, so I went back to my sewing machine. But I couldn't help thinking about something that had happened the other day.

It was Sunday afternoon. I was coming past the corner barbershop when I spotted Babbo with Zi' Vincenzo, Audenzio, and other men. Curious, I stooped down outside the doorway, my head hidden, as if to tie my shoe.

Babbo was talking. I only caught the end of his sentence, something about "the Industrial Workers of the World."

I wondered if this is a different union for Italian workers. I wanted to hear more. Audenzio bent forward as if he were about to argue something in return. At that moment, he glanced outside and spotted me. For a second, our eyes met. I straightened up and rushed on.

I'm almost certain now that *mio padre* and his friends have long discussions about workers and unions, but it seems as though these unions are different from the ones the Jewish workers belong to.

What does Babbo think about all of this? I wish I knew.

Friday, November 19, 1909

Tonight after work a man on the street thrust a flyer into my hand. He had stacks to hand out — not just in Yiddish, either. Some were in Italian, and others in English. The flyer was about the meeting next Monday night at the Cooper Union building.

"Oh, Angela. For a girl who has been to school, you don't seem to have brains. Think about it — what good will a strike do?" cried Luisa when I showed it to her. "This is only for Jewish girls. They will lose, anyway. The factory owners are too powerful."

I took a breath and tried to repeat the arguments I've heard Sarah make. "Luisa, it's because the factory owners are so powerful that we must all act together. Sarah says that as long as only one or two factories are on strike, nothing will change. Everyone must join together."

But Luisa turned on me. "'Sarah says, Sarah says!' Angela, what have I been telling you? Don't listen to Sarah Goldstein! The leaders of this union haven't even tried to talk to us. They don't care about Italian girls."

When Sarah talks about fighting for our rights, she makes me want to listen and join in. But then I listen to Luisa, and I can't help wondering why there aren't more Italians leading the union, especially if it is supposed to be for all workers.

I feel more confused than ever.

Tuesday, November 23, 1909

I have so much to write about! I'll start at the beginning, when I opened my eyes. Of course the first thing I thought of was last night's meeting. I couldn't wait to find out the news from Sarah.

Luisa, Rosa, and I rushed to work without speaking. The weather is colder now, and the wind seeps through my coat and makes me shiver. But as soon as the shop came into sight and I spotted Sarah waiting for me, I forgot all about being cold.

I hung back so I could talk to her. Luisa shot me an angry look and pounded up the stairs. "Hurry, or you'll be late, Angela."

Sarah and I lingered in the dim hall. She was eager to tell me everything. The "Great Hall" at Cooper Union had been so packed, she said, that some people had to stand outside in the street. Her words rushed out. She told me about the labor leaders who spoke, like Samuel Gompers and Mary Dreier, the leader of the WTUL.

Sarah leaned forward and put her hand on my coat sleeve. "After two hours of speeches, no one had called for a strike. Instead, each speaker warned us not to enter into a strike hastily."

I frowned. "So that's it? No strike?"

A quick smile lit Sarah's face. "Wait, I'm not finished. Just when it seemed the meeting would end, a young woman named Clara Lemlich shouted that she wanted to speak. She was lifted to the stage on the shoulders of other workers."

Sarah said that Clara Lemlich works in the Leiserson shop, which is already on strike. Earlier this fall, Clara was beaten on the picket line by thugs the factory owners hired to bother the girls.

Sarah's eyes flashed. "When Clara stood on that stage, she seemed to speak for all of us. She said we must break the bonds that hold us."

I could picture Sarah herself speaking before a huge

crowd, moving people to tears with her powerful words. I think she could do just as well as this Clara Lemlich.

Sarah said that when Clara called for a general strike of all shirtwaist workers, the crowd went wild. It was the moment the workers had been waiting for. Everyone took the old Jewish oath. "We said it in Yiddish, Angela, but we strike together — Jewish girls, Americans, and Italians," Sarah told me.

She raised her right hand and recited the oath for me. " 'If I turn traitor to the cause I now pledge, may this hand wither from the arm I now raise.' "

Her words made me shiver. "What will happen now?" I asked.

"I promise you, Angela, something *will* happen this morning," Sarah replied. "Don't put your hat in your locker this morning. Keep your coat right beside you."

Minutes later, I could feel my fingers begin to tremble with excitement as I lined up the seam on my first shirtwaist. The power was turned on. Vroom! The room sprang to life with the noise of the sewing machines. The floor vibrated under my feet.

I bent to my work. Everything seemed as usual. But it was not. I knew it, Sarah knew it. I think Luisa did, too, for by then, everyone had heard the whispered story of last night. I could hardly keep sewing straight seams.

We worked for two hours. There was only the sound of the machines and Mr. Klein's voice, urging us to work faster.

Just when I decided nothing would happen after all, something did. I thought it would be Sarah who would call the strike. But it was a girl named Ruth, who sat near me.

Around ten o'clock, Ruth stood up, took a whistle from her pocket, and blew it. It made a thin, screeching sound. I was so startled, I jumped in my chair.

In a clear voice, Ruth yelled, "I now declare a strike in this shop!"

The machines were roaring, so she called out the words again, even more loudly. Then she leaped onto a chair and reached up to a switch on the wall. My heart beat faster when I saw what she meant to do. She didn't hesitate for an instant. She turned off the electric current.

All together we rose up out of our seats. Mr. Klein began to wave his arms and yell, "Girls! Sit down! Sit down!"

No one listened. Without a word, we took our coats and hats. And we all walked out. Even Luisa and Rosa.

Later

Mama is about to turn off the gaslight for bed, but I have a few more minutes. My mind is still racing about everything that happened today. My pen has to chase my thoughts across the page!

After we stopped our machines, we ran downstairs and into the street. In front of our building I saw a policeman with a club. He shook it at us and yelled. The other girls didn't pay a bit of attention. But I couldn't help looking over my shoulder, worried that a policeman or even Mr. Klein would come after us.

Sarah laughed and linked her arm through mine. "Don't be afraid, Angela. Mr. Klein can't stop us. Look around you. There are thousands of girls here, from every shop on this street, from all over the neighborhood."

It was true. The streets were full of working girls. It looked like quitting time, but it was only ten in the morning. I stood on tiptoes to find Luisa, but I'd lost her and Rosa in the crowd.

At first I thought we would just go home. But I soon found out differently. Clara came up and took my other arm. "Let's all walk to strike headquarters on Clinton Street together."

Sarah nodded. "Yes, you *must* join the union now, Angela."

Join the union! I sputtered. "But . . . but . . . how can I? I must find my sister!"

I craned my neck and yelled, "Luisa!"

Sarah pointed. "Don't worry, she's over there with your friend Rosa. See? Just ahead. Come on."

Around me, girls shouted and sang, waving their arms in the air. I couldn't help being swept up in the crowd. I wondered if Luisa was feeling this excitement, too. I thought that maybe, now that the strike was actually happening, she might change her mind about Sarah and the union.

Sarah was laughing. "Do you believe this, Angela? We've filled the streets!"

We made our way to Clinton Hall, a large building on Clinton near Broome Street. Everywhere, I saw dark skirts and white shirtwaists and hats. Sarah steered me through the crowd, and eventually we stood before a desk where a girl asked if I was ready to join the union.

"She is! Aren't you, Angela?" asked Sarah. "Here's a dime to get you started. Her name is Angela Denoto."

I hesitated and tried to step back, but there were girls on every side of me. Before I could speak, the girl had taken down my name. It would be a dollar and fifty cents in all, she explained, but the rest could be paid later. And then I was pushed ahead.

My thoughts were all jumbled. What would my parents say? But then I told myself that I hadn't really joined. After all, it was Sarah's dime, not mine. I wouldn't really be a full member unless I paid the whole amount.

There was a crush of girls around me. Most were yelling and calling out to one another in Yiddish. But I saw some Americans and a few Italian girls, too. I made for the door. Outside, I spotted Luisa and Rosa at last.

Luisa pushed her way through the crowd and grabbed my arm so hard, it hurt. "Where have you been? We've been looking all over for you. Let's go home."

"But . . . but don't you think we should stay here with everyone else?" I managed to say.

Rosa leaned over and put her arm around me. "Angela, our shop will likely settle soon. We'll probably go back to work in a few days — a week at the most. If not, we'll find work elsewhere. A strike might be all right for the Jewish girls, but our families need our wages too much, don't they?"

I stared at Rosa and Luisa. I didn't know what to say.

Sarah came up behind me. "Come back inside, Angela. The speeches are starting. The union leaders will explain about how to picket and what we're all fighting for. We must stick together. It's the only way we can change things."

"What's she saying?" Rosa asked. "Does she want you to go back inside?"

Sarah had spoken in English so quickly, Luisa and Rosa couldn't understand everything. I stared at Luisa. So many thoughts flew through my mind. Luisa glared, her lips set in a hard line, her eyes flashing. She looked as if she wanted to slap my face.

All at once, Luisa grabbed Rosa's arm and stomped away, disappearing into the crowd.

I stood on the sidewalk for a long moment. I knew I should run after them. But, more than anything, I wanted to stay with Sarah and the other fiery girls. I wanted to be a part of the struggle for our rights.

Even now, I can hardly believe my own boldness. But I turned and followed Sarah back into Clinton Hall.

Later, after all the speeches, I raced home along Broome all the way to Elizabeth Street. As my feet hit the tenement stairs, I got a hard knot in my stomach. I tiptoed past Zi' Maria's door — it would be just like her to pull me in and ask me questions!

Everything seemed as usual, at first. Mama was cooking macaroni. Luisa was at the table with Vito, who was ignoring his homework, bragging about all the wood he'd scavenged after school. Teresa smiled when she saw me. "Angela, help me with my arithmetic," she begged.

Babbo came in just before our meal. I could hardly touch my food.

At last, Luisa took a deep breath. "You've heard about this strike of the workers. But don't worry, Mama, as soon as there is a chance to go back to work, we will take it."

Babbo pointed his fork at Luisa. "Did you go to the union hall today, like Angela?"

"No, Babbo, I did not!" cried Luisa.

I hung my head then, waiting to be punished. Of course Mama and Babbo already knew I had been at Clinton Hall. Nothing can be kept secret here! Other girls from Elizabeth Street were out of work, too. Probably someone at the barbershop had told *mio padre* I'd been seen at strike headquarters.

Then something surprising happened. Babbo began to shoot questions at me. He asked how strong the union was, how many workers had walked off the job, how many Italian girls had been at the meeting hall.

I swallowed hard and answered as best I could. Mama went to the sink and began clattering dishes. Teresa took out her homework and pretended to study, while Vito kept shoveling in his macaroni. Luisa sat with her arms folded across her chest, her face flushed with anger.

When I finished, there was silence. We waited for Babbo to speak. If he forbade me to go back to the union hall, there was nothing to be done.

For a long moment I stared down at the bright colors of the oilcloth Mama had put on the table. She's always done her best to make our apartment cheerful, even when money is scarce. I swallowed hard. Now where will the money come from?

Babbo got up, rubbing his shoulder. He turned to Mama and said in the words of our village back home, "There are many who do not trust this union. It is getting help from rich American ladies."

He paused, then added, "Yet young Audenzio says there are some in his cloakmakers' shop who are closely watching what happens here. We will have to see. . . ."

At the door, he turned and said to me, "For now, be careful."

Mama banged her cooking pot after he left. Keeping her back to us, she shook her head. "*Sì*, you must be careful. Who knows what can happen here? No doubt there will soon be a chance to go back to work."

Luisa got up and said she would go visit Rosa. She left quickly, shutting the door hard behind her.

My heart was beating fast. It's just begun, but already I feel that the strike is tearing my family apart.

Still, I couldn't help feeling more excited than I ever had. For Babbo hadn't said no! He hadn't told me not to join the union, he hadn't said I couldn't listen to speeches.

And so I'm going back.

Friday, November 26, 1909

Today didn't begin well. Luisa and I fought again. Teresa was sleeping deeply beside me, her breathing slow and even, but I knew Luisa, like me, had tossed and turned most of the night.

Luisa's hoarse whisper broke the silence. "Angela, maybe you believe those fiery girls can change things and make life better for working girls. But use your eyes and look around. You'll see — nothing is going to change. We'll be back to work in a day or two, and all of this will be forgotten. Mama needs us."

I didn't know how to answer. So I got dressed and left.

Clinton Hall was crackling with noise and chatter. There were crowds of girls everywhere.

I pressed into a corner to listen to what people were saying. Most of the girls were speaking in Yiddish and

English. Here and there, I spotted a few Italian girls like me. Speeches were going on all the time, with girls cheering and clapping.

"The bosses only want you for your hands," I heard one woman say. "Not for your heads or your hearts."

I found myself nodding as I listened. That was true. I've seen signs that say simply, HANDS WANTED. I think we are like that horse I saw, who was used until she was all worn out.

At last I spotted Sarah and Clara. Sarah was so excited, she grabbed my hands and practically twirled me around. "Twenty thousand girls are on strike, Angela!" she cried, her words tumbling out. "Most of the labor leaders — the men, anyway — thought there wouldn't be more than five thousand. Now we must seize this chance and stand firm. If we give in, it'll be easy for the larger shops, like the Triangle Waist Company, to ignore our demands. Those Triangle owners are so powerful, they'll do whatever they can to fight the strike."

Near us, two WTUL ladies with fancy hats were talking. I couldn't help wondering if Mama had made the flowers on those hats. I heard one woman say, "We have the Italian girls in a hall nearby, but we need Italian speakers or we will lose them. Oh, where are the Italian speakers?"

The lady beside her shook her head. "Six hundred waist and dress shops, but we have no Italian organizers! Is there no one?"

Sarah had heard, too. Before I knew it, she had pushed me forward. Sarah told the union lady that I was Italian, and that my English was good, too.

The lady's eyes lit up. "Is this true? What's your name, dear? Have you been to school? We desperately need someone to translate for some of the Italian girls. We must explain to them why it's important not to cross the picket lines, not to be scabs."

I told her my name and said I had been to school for four years.

"Marvelous! Come with me, and report here every day. We can use you." She grabbed my arm and led me away. As we walked, she told me how important it was for the workers to know the progress of the strike and the rules for picketing. So girls who are fluent in Yiddish, English, and Italian are needed to translate.

The union lady took me to a cold, dingy hall nearby. As the union leaders made announcements in English, I repeated the words in Italian as best I could. Then I translated the girls' questions into English so the union ladies could answer them.

At first I was nervous and spoke too softly. Girls in the

back of the room clamored for me to speak up. But it wasn't long before I got used to standing in front of the crowded room.

Once, someone shouted, "That girl is too short. Give her a box to stand on!" Everyone laughed.

So now I have become not only a striking worker, but a speaker.

Monday, November 29, 1909

This morning Babbo left the tenement just as I did. We walked to the corner, where the pushcart vendors were setting up for the day.

"The headquarters are on Clinton Street, Babbo," I told him, when we reached Broome Street, where I would turn.

Babbo nodded. "You look like your mama these days, Angela. When you were a baby back in Sicily, she helped storm the city council office to protest against taxes. It must be in your blood."

I could hardly believe my ears. Mama had been involved in a tax revolt? I wanted to ask more, but Babbo had to rush off to his job. I wonder if he'd ever been part of a protest or strike back in Sicily, too. Maybe that's what they talk about in the barbershop. And maybe that's why

Babbo — and Mama — are letting me take part in the strike . . . for now, at least.

Today, Clinton Hall reminded me of a beehive. People buzzed and chattered, flying here and there. Oh, and the speeches!

Clara Lemlich spoke this morning. She's the one Sarah told me about, who helped start the strike. She's not even twenty years old, yet she can speak to a large crowd and move people to tears.

My voice got hoarse from translating in a loud voice, and from cheering. At one point Clara cried, "If we stick together — and we are going to stick together — we will win!" The room burst into applause. With such spirit, how can we lose?

Sarah seems to be everywhere, encouraging girls and handing out assignments for the picket line. She and Clara Ruben plan to join the picket line soon, and Sarah wants me to join them.

"Angela, we must have an Italian girl and a Jewish girl walking side by side. We must!" Sarah cried.

I felt my heart lurch, and I didn't answer. Going to the union hall and translating speeches is one thing. But walking the picket line . . . ?

Everyone knows the factory owners send rough men and women to harass and scare the strikers. They've been doing it all fall with the smaller factory strikes. I remember that Sarah told me Clara Lemlich was beaten. Others have been arrested and sent to jail, and even the workhouse.

No, I don't think I'm brave enough for that.

Tuesday, November 30, 1909

Today one of the union ladies asked me to take a message to the girls picketing outside the Leiserson shop.

When I got there, the workers were walking peacefully up and down with their signs. But then several rough-looking men appeared. They began to abuse the girls, calling them bad names and telling them to go home. My face got red just listening to them. I kept expecting the policeman who was standing nearby to say something to stop them, but he did nothing. Nothing at all!

How can we win this strike when everyone is against us?

When I got home, Mama sent me to the bakery to get bread. I was glad for the chance to see Arturo again. He looked up with his warm smile.

"Angela, I heard you're with the Jewish girls in this

strike," he said as I chose a nice large Sicilian loaf with a thick crust.

I sighed. "It seems there are no secrets on Elizabeth Street."

"My sister Tina started work at the Triangle Waist Company a few weeks ago," Arturo went on. "She still has her job there. Perhaps you could get one, too. I know your family depends on Luisa and you to put bread on the table."

I mumbled, *"Grazie,"* took my bread, and left. I walked home slowly, hardly noticing the crowds around me. The bread felt heavy and leaden in my hands. All the excitement of the day seemed to drain away.

I'm so confused. One part of me knows that Arturo is right. He was just being kind to suggest that I work at the Triangle factory. Because no matter what Clara Lemlich and Sarah and all the union ladies say, the longer the strike continues, the harder it will be not to become a scab — to go back to work and break the strike. After all, even though Mama protested a tax back in Sicily, that was years ago. How patient will she be with this strike when the rent is due, and we need money for food?

Still, if I look into my heart, I know there is a part of me that would rather starve than give up this struggle.

Thursday, December 2, 1909

Today I heard a red-haired girl named Rose Schneiderman speak. Her words made me think again about that loaf of bread I carried home from Arturo's bakery.

Rose said our struggle is not only about getting a loaf of bread. She said a union helps us realize that the hurt of one is the concern of all. If we have decent working conditions, then we can have other things in life, too. Like time to go to night school to improve our lives.

I'd never thought of it like that before. But I know Sarah believes this strongly. That's why she was able to stand up and take action that day Clara hurt her hand — even if it meant risking her own job.

I wonder: Can I ever be as brave as that?

Speaking of being brave, we heard that a policeman hit one of the strikers yesterday. The union leaders say it's because the owners have hired thugs, like those rough-looking men I saw, to break up the picket lines. Not only that, police officers have been bribed or "sugared" to support the cause of the owners. I guess that's why the police officer I saw did nothing to help the strikers. This isn't right! Police officers shouldn't take money and hurt innocent girls.

Tomorrow there'll be a march to city hall to complain

about the police officers. Sarah wants me to go, but I must stay home to help Mama make flowers. After all, I have to make up for not working somehow.

It's so cold now. Mama burned only three bushels of coal in the kitchen stove this week. That comes to seventy-five cents for cooking and heating both. If both Luisa and I were working, we could probably buy five bushels a week, enough to keep all our three rooms warmer. Mama has been keeping Teresa home from school to help her and Zi' Maria make flowers during the day. I wish our apartment were warmer. Teresa gets colds so easily this time of year.

I took Vito aside tonight and asked him to try to find more wood and old packing boxes from the streets that Mama can burn in the stove.

"I will, Angela. But when are you going back to work?" he said.

"Soon," I promised.

Vito said nothing. But his look made me cringe. I think he's against the strike, too.

Sunday, December 5, 1909

Today I went to my first workers' rally. I'll never forget it!

First I walked to Sarah's tenement building on Orchard

Street. She was waiting for me outside, then we walked to the rally. By two o'clock, thousands of people were lined up. I heard one policeman say eight thousand people were there.

The speeches were so inspiring. My favorite was Publio Mazzella's, who spoke in Italian. He urged us not to give up, and said the Italians should do more to organize. I felt proud to see an Italian onstage with the other leaders.

I also liked the speech by the Reverend Anna Shaw. She said, "You can't strike a blow with one finger or two fingers, but when you want to strike you put all your fingers together, clench them hard and let them drive. That's what the workers must do with themselves."

I walked Sarah back to Orchard Street. All the good smells from the pushcarts tickled my nose and made my stomach growl. There were roasting chestnuts, steaming hot sweet potatoes, and warm, crusty bread.

I am hungry almost all the time now. Sarah is, too. She says she misses the food she loves: cabbage and gefilte fish. Those are Jewish foods I don't eat, but I do love steaming sweet potatoes from a cart.

But after listening to the speeches today, Sarah says she doesn't care about food anymore. "Angela, we must work harder and not give up trying to get better hours, more pay, and more rights. We are already starving, slaving away in these shops and factories. So this should be our new slogan: 'We'd rather starve quickly than starve slowly.'"

I thought about Sarah's words as I walked home, past all the pushcarts. It's fine for Sarah and me. But what about Teresa?

Tuesday, December 7, 1909

Today was a hard day. Sarah and Clara were not in the union hall at all. I know where they were — on the picket line.

Then tonight, Luisa and I fought again. I was telling her about a man named Arturo Caroti, who's begun to visit Italian families to explain about the strike and get their support.

Luisa shook her head. "Don't let him come here, Angela! I'm tired of waiting for our shop to settle. This has gone on long enough. Mama needs my full pay. I don't care if I do have to cross the picket lines. Rosa and I are hoping to start new jobs at the Triangle Waist Company any day now."

The Triangle factory! I didn't know what to say. The worst part is, unless our shop settles soon, Mama will expect me to get a job there, too. I hope she'll let me wait a little longer.

Besides, as I've told Mama, the Triangle factory has many workers. Since I'm only fourteen, I probably would have to go back to snipping threads instead of being a machine operator. I would be better off and would make more money in our smaller shop. I just hope ours settles soon!

Wednesday, December 8, 1909

I looked everywhere, but Sarah and Clara weren't in the union hall again this morning.

In the late afternoon, one of the union ladies came up to me. "Aren't you Sarah Goldstein's Italian friend? We just found out she was arrested on the picket line."

I asked if Sarah had been hurt, but the lady shrugged. She didn't know. It would be just like Sarah to be bold and call attention to herself. What if she's been beaten?

Thursday, December 9, 1909

I got to Clinton Hall early and searched frantically for Sarah. Finally, in the afternoon, I saw her come through the door. Clara, too. I ran and hugged them both.

Sarah said that a tall, fat policeman with a red face had

yelled at the picketers to go home and mind their own business.

"An Italian girl came out of the shop we were picketing," Sarah said. "We told her the shop was on strike and asked her to join the union. Then one of the thugs the bosses hired came over. He hit me so hard, I fell down."

Clara nodded. "The policeman saw the whole thing, so I asked him to help us. He told us to come to the station to testify against the thug. But when we got there, *we* were the ones treated like criminals."

Sarah said they were thrown into a cell with some drunken women. When their case came up in the court, the boss of the shop and the Italian girl testified against them. They lied, saying that Sarah had hit the Italian girl and called her a scab.

It isn't fair! The workers have the right to strike. Why should the girls be treated like criminals and thrown into jail?

Sarah told me she was going back to the picket line. She begged, "Angela, come with me!"

But I didn't answer.

Monday, December 13, 1909

Well, it happened! Luisa and Rosa have jobs at the Triangle Waist Company. They started this morning. If our shop doesn't settle soon, I will be forced to join them.

I must have hope. After all, more and more of the smaller shops are agreeing to the union's demands. Many girls have already gone back to work.

Still, it seems odd that on the day my sister became a scab, I was asked to read the rules for strikers to some Italian girls. Of course, I already know them by heart.

Rules for Pickets

Don't walk in groups of more than two or three.

Don't stand in front of the shop; walk up and down the block.

Don't stop the person you wish to talk to; walk alongside of her.

Don't get excited and shout when you are talking.

Don't put your hand on the person you are speaking to.

Don't call anyone "scab" or use abusive language of any kind.

Plead, persuade, appeal, but do not threaten.

If a policeman arrests you and you are sure that

you have committed no offense, take down his number and give it to your union officers.

Tuesday, December 14, 1909

This morning when I went to the union hall, an American WTUL said, "Please come with me. Today we need someone on the picket line who speaks Italian, someone who can convince the Italian girls not to break the strike."

She seemed so calm and confident that I would do it that I found myself following her. Sarah came, too. We stood on the sidewalk outside a shop with some other girls and waited. Soon we saw an Italian man leading some girls into the building, through our picket lines.

I cried out in Italian, "Please, do not break the strike. We must stand together to help everyone."

The girls kept walking. The man scowled at me. I cannot be angry with them, though some of the other strikers are. Maybe it's because I know how hard it is for them. I know their parents depend on these girls for food and rent money. I know they watch their fathers work like dogs, at jobs that often pay less than their own. And I know they have little sisters, like mine, who walk to school shivering in thin coats.

• • •

Tonight Luisa told me she likes the Triangle factory. She said they play music at lunch.

I didn't dare tell her about the picket line.

Wednesday, December 15, 1909

I walked on the picket line again today. I'm getting more used to it. I guess it's easier than I thought to be brave.

Today I was more cold than scared. Before long, my fingers and toes were numb and the tips of my ears began to sting. But at least nothing bad happened.

When I got home I finally found out what Vito is up to. He has quit school, even though he's still thirteen. He's going to work as a shoeshine boy.

"I've been selling rags and scraps of wood for weeks," Vito announced, throwing his shoulders back proudly. "Finally I got enough to buy a shoeshine kit. This is just the beginning. Someday I'll be a rich businessman!"

"Then you can buy me all the candy I can eat," said Teresa. Poor Teresa, she hasn't had even one piece of candy for such a long time.

Even though I wish he could have stayed in school, I'm proud of my little brother.

Now Teresa is the only one left at school, but she stays

home a lot to help Mama make flowers. Each night I look at Teresa's thin face and listen to her rough breathing beside me. She needs more good food and warm clothes. It seems as if her wheezing is getting worse. Sometimes I feel it is my fault that she's suffering.

Oh, I hope our shop settles soon.

Later

Mama has just come to talk to me. I was sitting at the kitchen table, writing in my book. She was on her way to the toilet in the hall and said she would be shutting off the gaslight as soon as she came back.

"*Sì*, Mama," I told her. "I am almost done writing."

Then Mama did a surprising thing. She came to stand by my shoulder and said in a soft voice, "Your *padre* is right, Angela. You must be careful in this strike. We've heard the stories of policemen attacking workers on the picket line. I will bring my rolling pin and fight them off if they threaten you!"

"Oh, Mama! I am safe, don't worry." But I can't help smiling at the thought of my mama with her long skirt and shawl, holding a rolling pin under her arm and waving it in the face of a burly policeman.

I feel that Mama, more than Babbo, would just as soon I forget about the strike and go back to work. But I am thankful she has not forced me to — yet.

Maybe she remembers those times back home when she fought, too. Even though my parents don't trust this union, it seems they remember what it is like to fight for justice.

Sometimes I hear girls in the factory talking about how old-fashioned their parents are, how foreign they are, and how they don't understand what it is to be American. Our teachers in school don't seem to pay them much respect, either. I don't think Miss Kelly really understood what courage it took for my family to leave everything behind and come here.

But somehow this strike is making me open my eyes and imagine Mama and Babbo as different people. Oh, here is Mama's hand on the doorknob; time to go to bed.

Monday, December 20, 1909

Good news today. Seven thousand shirtwaist workers in Philadelphia have gone on strike. They refused to do work sent to them by garment factories here in New York City.

There is bad news, too. More and more girls are crossing the picket lines to go back to work. And many of them are Italian girls. This morning I stood outside one shop and called on two girls to please stop. But they hurried by without even looking at me. My voice is getting hoarse.

Sarah is angry when she sees scabs. But my heart isn't bitter. I understand.

Also, Italian girls and their families weren't involved in planning the strike at the beginning. Sometimes it makes me angry to hear the union ladies blame the Italian girls for being weak and for not caring about the strike. But things aren't so simple.

Sarah has the support of her family because they've been involved in this union, or one like it. But if the families haven't been involved, what can the girls do?

I think it's a good thing that Arturo Caroti and another man, Salvatore Ninfo, are trying to keep the Italian girls from crossing the picket lines by going from house to house to talk to the families and pay strike relief. Still, these Italian organizers should have been part of the fight weeks ago.

Later

Well, right after I wrote these words in my diary I heard more about the Italian labor leader Caroti. Mama sent me to take some of her fresh macaroni to Rosa's family. What a surprise I had when I walked in, for there at the table was Zi' Vincenzo, along with my papa and Rosa's boyfriend,

Audenzio. They were in the midst of a loud discussion and barely noticed me come in.

"They've recruited Arturo Caroti to help in the shirt-waist strike," Zi' Vincenzo was saying in a disgusted voice, pounding his fist on the table. "But that's only because he helped lead striking silk workers in New Jersey last month. Why didn't they come to the Italian community earlier? I tell you, we can't trust these American labor unions."

I started. They were talking about our strike! I wanted to sit down at the table and join in. But that wouldn't do, in a room full of men.

Instead, I walked as slowly and quietly as I could across the kitchen, placing the bowl of macaroni on a small table in the corner. Out of the corner of my eye I saw a move-ment. Audenzio was starting to speak and, just as he had done in the barbershop, he began to gesture wildly.

"True, true," he cried. "Still, here in New York, we must find ways to combine forces with the Jewish labor leaders. The men miscalculated the determination of these girls. Local 25 of the ILGWU is disorganized, they didn't plan well enough. It's clear these girls will fail, even with the help of those Americans from the WTUL, the Women's Trade Union League. But we can learn from their mistakes. This shirtwaist strike may do more than expected. It may help us down the road if we learn from it."

Fail! In spite of myself, I whirled around to stare at Audenzio. Who did he think he was? He was talking about the strike as if it were already over! How dare he speak so calmly of our certain defeat? He wasn't out on the picket line in the cold. He wasn't sacrificing for his family.

At that moment, he looked up and our eyes met. I shot him a dark look that would have made Luisa proud.

Suddenly, Babbo, whose back was to me, turned. For the first time, he seemed to notice I was there. I quickly crossed to the door, mumbling something about Mama's gift of macaroni. Then I let myself out.

Well, it's a good thing Audenzio is Rosa's boyfriend, not Luisa's!

Monday, December 27, 1909

What an awful day! More strikers were arrested. Thugs came outside the shop where we were picketing. They knocked some of the girls to their knees, striking at them. I was afraid, and stepped to the back. I began to tremble. I didn't want to be beaten by these rough-looking men.

The thugs made a path for the scabs, who ran to the door of the factory with their eyes straight ahead. I think they were ashamed to look at us.

It is always the same story. Even though we were the

ones who were attacked, when the police came they arrested strikers, not the thugs!

Sarah had bad news today, too. From the moment I first saw her I just knew something had happened. Clara has begun working at the Triangle Waist Company!

"I cannot believe she would do this," she kept repeating over and over.

"You can't blame her, Sarah," I told her. "Clara's the only support for her mother. It's not her fault she couldn't hold out any longer. I don't blame Rosa or Luisa, either."

But Sarah has a special hatred for the Triangle factory, partly because she once worked there, but mostly because it's one of the larger factories that are resisting the union the most. The big bosses at Triangle are Isaac Harris and Max Blanck, Sarah told me. They're known as "the shirtwaist kings."

Girls are going to work there because they are desperate. "But these bosses will *never* agree to all the union demands, like better fire escapes and no locked doors," Sarah said, her voice bitter and tired.

I told Sarah what Luisa had said, that at the Triangle factory she gets hot tea at lunch, and even phonograph music. Sarah just shook her head. "Just wait, Angela. I know this factory. They won't be serving tea once this strike is over."

Tuesday, December 28, 1909

There was more trouble today. Our union, Local 25 of the ILGWU, rejected an agreement with the largest companies, which are part of the Associated Waist and Dress Manufacturers. These companies said they would agree to some of our demands, like a fifty-two-hour work week and no charges for needles and supplies. But they refused to recognize the union or accept the union's role.

Some of the rich American ladies from the WTUL, who have been helping us, think that Local 25 should have accepted this offer, because it gives us some of the things we want. They say it was our best chance, and we'll lose public sympathy by turning it down.

But if the companies don't agree that the union's role is to bargain for all workers, then we lose in the end, anyway. The companies want an open shop — they want to be able to hire union and non-union workers. But we want a closed shop — only union workers. If we give in to the open shop, we'll never have the power to force them to change.

Sometimes when I look at what I have written in this book, I feel so surprised. Just a few months ago, I was in school. I'd never even heard of a labor union. Now I'm learning about unions, closed shops, open shops, and the rights of workers. I've even spoken in front of rooms full of girls.

I wonder what Miss Kelly would say about her little sparrow now.

Wednesday, December 29, 1909

Today I sold newspapers! It was a special edition of the worker newspaper, *The Call*, to benefit the strikers. I wore a white ribbon like a sash and stood on a cold street corner with Sarah and some other girls.

We sold all our papers in only two hours. Usually *The Call* costs two cents, but this special edition was a nickel. Some people gave even more than that! One man pressed a quarter into my hand and wished me good luck. Later on we heard that the strikers sold forty-five thousand newspapers.

"Even though we're stronger than anyone thought, the big companies are holding out," Sarah said today as we stood shivering in the wind. "I wonder if we'll be strong enough in the end."

Sarah is certain our shop will settle in just a few days. I hope so, for I can't hold out much longer. Luisa wants me to apply for a job at the Triangle factory. She likes it there, and says that since it's one of the larger shops, there will be work all year and that the workdays always end at six.

Sarah laughed when I told her this. "What have I told you? When the strike ends, those girls will be back to working until nine o'clock at night, except for Friday and Saturday. And there is no overtime pay. Do you know what they'll do instead? They'll give them a piece of apple pie. I'd rather have my money than pie!"

Sarah remembers a big sign posted at the Triangle factory on Saturday afternoons during the busy season. The sign read, IF YOU DON'T COME IN ON SUNDAY, YOU NEED NOT COME IN ON MONDAY.

Monday, January 3, 1910

It's a new year, but there's not much to celebrate. Mama needed me to make flowers today. Teresa helped, too. But it seems to me the shadows under her eyes have grown darker, and she coughs more than ever.

I helped Mama cook today. With our money so low, it is always pasta and beans, pasta and beans every day.

Maybe that's why each day there are fewer girls at the union hall. After all, everyone has to eat. But even though I feel like giving up, Sarah has remained firm. She's ready to fight to the end.

Sarah says that all her family eats now are potatoes. Sarah can make things seem funny even when they are sad. Today she even sang me a song about potatoes. The song was in Yiddish, so I didn't understand it, but Sarah translated it into English:

> Sunday, potatoes
> Monday, potatoes
> Tuesday and Wednesday, potatoes
> Thursday and Friday, potatoes
> Saturday we live to see a potato pudding,
> And Sunday we have potatoes again.

Tuesday, January 4, 1910

Well, the strike is over for me. Tonight Mama said it was time, we could not wait any longer. There's nothing I can do now. And so I promised that I'd go with Luisa to the Triangle factory on Monday.

We fought so hard, but every day, the number of girls out on strike is smaller. The girls and their families are hungry. And it's so cold, no one can stand to walk the picket lines for long. I saw a copy of *The Call* today. It says there is a cold wave starting, with bitter north winds blowing in.

Sarah says we should feel proud that we've come this far. And there *will* be changes in some of the small shops, like ours. But will these changes last?

I think that's the saddest part for me. Even after so many workers and their families sacrificed so much, we couldn't make the large factories change. Big factories like Triangle have stayed open the whole time with scabs. The Bijou Waist Company even brought in cot beds for the scab workers, so they could sleep there and not have to cross the picket lines.

The Triangle owners will still make the girls work long hours, and will not give a half day on Saturday. And they won't recognize the union.

I wonder, what will it take to *really* change things?

Thursday, January 6, 1910

Something unexpected has happened: Our shop has settled after all! Now I can go back to work tomorrow and I won't have to cross the picket lines to work at the Triangle factory. My old shop is closer to home, so I'm glad. Besides, I wouldn't like to work so high up, on the eighth and ninth floors of the Asch Building, where the Triangle factory is.

As soon as I heard the news, I ran home right away to

tell Mama. Poor Mama, she's been suffering in our cold apartment for weeks. She's had to wrap herself in two shawls. Most of the time, she goes to Zi' Maria's kitchen to work on artificial flowers with her, because it's warmer there.

Maybe now we'll have enough money to buy an extra bushel of coal for the stove. Not only that, we can buy more food and Teresa will stop wheezing so much.

It's only the middle of January, but I feel light somehow, as if it's already spring and I can sit out on my fire escape and write in this book.

Friday, January 14, 1910

Back at work! I didn't even mind seeing Mr. Klein today. I'm so glad to be helping my family again. Luisa is speaking to me, but I can tell she's still angry about the strike.

Mr. Klein doesn't seem much friendlier. But at least he let us leave on time tonight, even though he grumbled about it.

Monday, January 24, 1910

Most girls are back at work, so I think the strike will probably draw to a close any day now.

More than three hundred employers have signed the union contract, agreeing to a fifty-two-hour work week and a raise. Night work will be limited to two hours a day, and not more than two times a week. I'm glad about that! And during slack season, the work will be divided among workers, and not just given to a few girls. That means more girls can depend on their jobs. Oh, and here's another thing I'm glad about: We won't have to pay for our own needles anymore.

Sarah says she's pleased because more girls have joined the union. "Before the strike, Local 25 had less than a thousand members. Now there are more than twenty thousand," she said today at lunch. "Some of them will eventually drop out, but at least now we can really start to build for the future. No one thought women and girls could strike. But we proved that we can."

Sarah and I weren't the only ones talking about the strike at lunch. And we didn't even whisper. Before, if the bosses knew you belonged to the union, you could get fired. Well, those days are gone!

No matter what, I guess we have accomplished something: The union is here to stay.

Tuesday, February 15, 1910

Sarah showed me her copy of *The Call*. The headline read: "SHIRTWAIST STRIKE WON!" I'm so proud that I was part of the largest strike ever by women, the strike everyone calls the "Uprising of the Twenty Thousand."

Of course, Sarah's not totally satisfied. Even though more than three hundred shops have agreed to the strikers' demands, she's grumbling about the thirteen firms that did not agree to everything the union wanted. She thinks this means that our gains won't last long.

"If only we could have forced the big companies like Triangle to agree to our demands," she said over and over.

I tried to lift her spirits. I said we should be pleased that the strike was more of a success than people had expected. Mostly, though, I'm just glad to be able to bring Mama my pay envelope again.

Monday, February 21, 1910

Vito came home today with a bag of candy for Teresa. He bought it himself with his shoeshine money.

"I found a factory where I could get broken candy for ten cents a pound," he boasted.

Teresa smiled when she saw the candy, but she only ate one piece.

We have more food now, but Teresa doesn't seem to have much of an appetite. Sometimes at night I wake up four or five times listening to her gasping for air beside me. I can't wait for this long winter to be over. I just know things will be better when spring comes. Maybe I'll even start saving for a spring hat myself.

Saturday, February 26, 1910

A half day today! I like that. But I do *not* like this weather. When the temperature changes, it seems to bring even more coughs and fever. Teresa caught a cold and didn't go to school all week. And when I helped Mama cook a meal of eggs and potatoes, Teresa barely touched the food on her plate.

Sunday, March 6, 1910

Now I've caught a cold, too. My throat hurts and I ache all over. I hate how my head throbs whenever I move. Even though I had a blanket wrapped around me, I shivered all day.

Mama hovers, and even Zi' Maria, who always seems so nosy and disapproving, clucked over me like a mother hen and fed me spoonfuls of her special soup. I think they are especially anxious because, just last week, in a building on the next block, the Bentavigna baby died. I heard Babbo tell Mama that the father, Gandolfo, a fish peddler, is beside himself with grief at the loss of his son. Mama does not call it pneumonia, though. She says, 'amonia.

Later, tired from coughing, I tried to sit up to work at our small table and help with making flowers, but I felt so weak Mama sent me back to the folding bed and said I could write in my little book.

Teresa has a cough, but today she's the one who nursed *me*. She brought me water and washed my forehead with a cool cloth.

"Are you better, Angela?" she asked softly. "I don't like that you are sick, but I'm glad to have you home with me."

"Tomorrow I have to go back to work no matter how I feel," I told her.

"Maybe we will work in the same factory someday, Angela. At least that way we can be together more."

I shook my head. "No! If you keep going to school, someday you can become a shopgirl or a secretary. That would be better than a shirtwaist worker."

Teresa just shrugged her small shoulders. She doesn't

seem to care that much about school. She likes being home with Mama best.

Monday, March 7, 1910

I went to work today, even though I felt weak and tired. I'm tired of my job. At least during the strike, things were exciting. My English got better, too. But now it's the same thing again, sewing on the machine day after day.

And even though Sarah is my good friend, sometimes I miss Luisa and Rosa. Still, I'm not ready to leave this job to work at the Triangle factory.

Luisa's heart is still hardened against me. Last night in bed I tried to share my worries about Teresa with her. I whispered, "Luisa, did Teresa's breathing always sound so rough? Even the tea Mama makes and the cod-liver oil she gives her don't seem to help much."

Luisa didn't answer. Perhaps she was already asleep. These days she comes home just as tired as ever. But maybe she just pretended not to hear me. I know she thinks it's my fault that Teresa's breathing has gotten so bad this winter. Luisa believes if I'd only gone back to work earlier, Teresa would be strong and well now.

Luckily, it's already March. Spring isn't far off, and Teresa always feels better in the warm sunshine. And soon

I'll be able to sit on the fire escape, watch for my sparrow, and write in my book. I can hardly believe how many pages I've filled.

Saturday, March 12, 1910

I haven't had much time to write all week. When I got home from work on Tuesday, Teresa seemed to have caught a bad cold. When she breathes, I can hear a gurgling sound in her chest. And her cough sounds deep and harsh.

Yesterday Mama sent Vito to fetch the doctor. The doctor thinks it's not a cold at all, but bronchitis or pneumonia. I think pneumonia might be worse for Teresa, because she sometimes wheezes and breathes hard even when she doesn't have a cold. Still, Teresa is young. The doctor has given us medicine and recommends hot compresses. He thinks she can fight it off.

Thursday, March 17, 1910

I'm so worried about Teresa, I've been rushing home from work every day, and can hardly concentrate on my sewing when I'm at my machine.

Teresa is holding her own, though. Mama hardly leaves

her bedside. She has even moved Teresa into her bed, with its pretty flounce, the *turnialettu*, which hides the storage space under the bed. Babbo is sleeping in the kitchen with Vito. At least Vito has moved from sleeping across chairs to a folding bed on the floor. That was the first thing he persuaded Mama to buy with his shoeshine money.

I hope the picture of St. Francis over the bed protects Teresa. Zi' Maria says she is praying every night.

Still, when I listen to Teresa's breathing, I feel scared. Sometimes there's a long pause in between each breath. When that happens, I squeeze her hand and cry, "Teresa!" It's as though I have to remind her to take the next breath.

Tuesday, March 22, 1910

We have lost her. I can hardly bear to write the words.

Over the last few days, she suddenly got worse. And then, last night, I went to bed as usual, but sleep never came. Perhaps, somehow, I knew. I kept getting up and tiptoeing into the room, stepping over Vito and Babbo curled up uneasily on the folding bed in the kitchen.

Just before dawn, I peeked in once more. Mama was on a chair next to the bed. Poor Mama, she was so tired that she'd put her head down on the blanket and dozed off.

Teresa's breath came in ragged tugs, and then, in just moments, everything changed. Her chest, which had risen and fallen with effort, grew still. Her face became peaceful. Her breath whispered away, and she was gone.

I am writing this on the roof. It is nearly dark. Somehow we got through this first day. There was much that Mama needed me to do. But now I'm alone, and my throat hurts from crying.

It's not fair! She was only a little girl, and she fought so hard. I don't understand . . . I don't. . . .

Saturday, March 26, 1910

It's hard to write. We've had a lot to do, and the apartment has been full of *paesani.* Everyone brings food, but it seems the only one who can eat is Vito.

Still, it's a comfort to have people near. Especially for Mama. Without our *paesani* she would surely go out of her mind with grief. I think half of Elizabeth Street — and certainly everyone on our block — has been here.

Zi' Maria has barely left our apartment, arriving first thing in the morning to make coffee and cooking supper at night. Whenever I go by her, she reaches out and grabs me and presses me to her chest. That only makes me cry.

She tries to make me eat, but I can only swallow a few bites.

Babbo sits at the kitchen table, his head buried in his hands. He asks for coffee, but then forgets to drink it. Other times he goes off with Zi' Vincenzo. Once, he came home late, and I guessed he had been at the café.

Like Zi' Maria, Luisa hasn't left Mama's side. She cries on Mama's shoulder, but at night in our bed she turns her back to me. I feel her anger in the dark.

There is truly something bad between us now. It's as if she's turned against me. In her heart she blames me for what happened. Maybe she's right.

Later

It's getting dark. This is the worst time for me. I've slept next to Teresa since she was a baby. She used to curl up against me to get warm in the winter. When she couldn't sleep, I whispered stories and songs into her ear.

Now there is only emptiness. It scares me. I don't understand how such a terrible thing can happen.

Saturday, April 2, 1910

Today I ruined two shirtwaists. Sometimes my tears come over me like a shower.

Now it is the afternoon and I am home. I can't write anymore. Mama needs me to go to the market for her.

At the bakery, Arturo gave me my bread, then reached out and took my hand to say how sorry he was about my sister. I could only nod. I ran out before I started to cry in front of him.

Friday, April 8, 1910

Last night I dreamed of Teresa. We were sitting at the table making artificial flowers. It was just the two of us. Teresa said, "Angela, look how quickly I can make daisies!"

And when I looked, her fingers had turned to butterflies.

I reached over to touch them, but at that moment, I woke up. It was still dark. I was sweating, and my cheeks were wet with tears.

Teresa seemed so real. Mama believes she is in heaven now. I must believe that, too.

Saturday, April 16, 1910

Every night I sit with Mama so she won't be alone. The days are hard for her without Teresa. At least after school Pietro and Alfio usually come to our apartment. Or they play outside on the street below, with Zi' Maria and Mama shouting out to them every so often.

This helps Rosa and Zi' Vincenzo, too, who is working long hours now that the construction season is busy. And it seems to makes Mama feel less lonely. Alfio loves to be with Mama and cries when it is time to leave. I think he still misses his own mother.

Today I took Alfio with me to get bread at the bakery. Arturo smiled me. He asked how my family was doing.

I answered as best I could. But just seeing Arturo's warm smile made me think of that day, long ago, when Teresa teased me about his being my boyfriend.

Alfio wanted to run off ahead of me on the way home. But I kept his small hand in mine and made him stay close. "After all, I am your 'little mother' today, Alfio," I told him, planting a kiss on the top of his head.

Monday, May 9, 1910

The days go by, but I don't seem to have the energy to write in my book. What does it matter if I fill it up? Miss Kelly probably doesn't even remember me now.

Our apartment seems so empty now without Teresa. When I trudge up the grimy stairs and open the door, I keep thinking I will see her sitting at the little kitchen table with Mama, making flowers with her small butterfly fingers.

I spend all my time with Mama. Luisa barely talks to me. Vito is gone most of the time, putting in long hours as a shoeshine boy. I know he gives Mama money every week, but I suspect he's keeping some back for himself, too.

It's spring now. The air is warm and the sun shines brightly. Soon the pushcarts will be bursting with wonderful fruits and spring greens. Today I even saw my sparrow on the fire escape. He hopped about as usual. He doesn't realize how everything has changed.

This year spring came too late.

Saturday, May 14, 1910

I think Sarah feels sorry for me. We haven't talked much lately at work. Sometimes I just go outside for a few minutes to be alone. Most of the girls in the shop can only talk about the new spring hats they want to buy.

Of course, Sarah's not like that. Still, as I told her, after all that has happened, it's hard to talk or care about ordinary things. Today, though, she asked me to walk to Washington Square after work. She thought it would be nice to meet Clara at five o'clock, and I could meet Luisa and Rosa, and walk in the park. But I told her no. I don't think my sister really cares about seeing me.

Then, on my way home, something odd happened. I saw an American man with a large camera on Elizabeth Street. He was taking photographs of people shopping in the market. I watched him for the longest time. I wonder if I'll be in a photograph myself.

It is strange to think about photographs. I wish we had one of Teresa. Zi' Maria has a portrait of her husband and herself, proudly displayed on a lace cloth on a shelf in her kitchen. It was taken just a year before her husband died in a construction accident. But when you look at his smile, it seems as if he could step out of the picture and say, *"Buon giorno."*

I wonder why this American man was taking photographs of the crowded streets of our neighborhood. He didn't ask for anyone's name. What will happen to these pictures?

I'd like to see myself in a photograph. Would I blend into the crowd, I wonder? Or would I stand out somehow as me, a real girl who lives on Elizabeth Street, a girl who is sad these days, and sometimes lonely. A girl who works hard and wonders what the future will hold.

Well, if I ever did see that photograph, I would grab a pencil and write "Angela Denoto" right over my head so people would know my name.

Saturday, May 21, 1910

Again today Sarah asked me to go with her after work to meet Clara. This time I went.

The Triangle factory doesn't get out as early as we do on Saturday afternoons, because it's not a union shop. So we stood outside the building and waited for Clara, Rosa, and Luisa. All I could think of was how much Teresa would have liked this warm spring day.

Luisa looked surprised to see me. Rosa smiled right away and linked my arm in hers. The three of us walked together in the park.

We didn't speak much. Perhaps all our thoughts were the same.

Saturday, June 11, 1910

This afternoon Sarah and I went to the park at Washington Square again to wait for Luisa, Clara, and Rosa.

Clara greeted me warmly. "You're getting so tall and pretty, Angela! On your first day of work last fall, I thought you looked like a shy, scared child. Now you're becoming such a young woman."

I blushed and said good-bye as Sarah and Clara went off to the market on Hester Street.

"They are nice girls, no?" asked Rosa. Luisa only scowled.

Just then Rosa spotted Audenzio. His cloak shop is nearby, so he'd just finished work, too. Rosa's face lit up and her eyes shone when she saw him stroll across the grass. That made me smile. After losing her mama, Rosa deserves a little happiness.

I'm not sure what I think about Audenzio, though. He certainly talks a lot and seems to have an opinion about everything. I hope that after they're married, Rosa has a chance to get a word in now and then. I'm not sure I like his ideas, either. I still remember that night I heard him dismiss our shirtwaist strike as a failure.

Today all Audenzio could talk about was a possible strike of cloakmakers this summer. He says there are about sixty thousand workers, mostly men, who make cloaks, suits, and shirts. More than half are Jewish, but at least ten thousand are Italian.

The conditions in these shops aren't any better than in the shirtwaist factories. During the busy season, Audenzio has to work fourteen or even sixteen hours a day. He told us the workers plan on asking for a forty-eight-hour work week and double pay for overtime.

"Our strike won't be as unorganized as your shirtwaist workers' effort," Audenzio said, waving his hands in the air as usual. "And there'll be more funds to help the workers' families so people won't have to cross the picket line. We are going to shut this part of the garment industry down."

I bristled. There he was again, criticizing our fight. Before I knew it, the words were out of my mouth. "Don't forget, the girls in our strike didn't have much support from the men who were the union leaders. At least the shirtwaist workers proved that women have the ability to fight."

Audenzio turned and looked at me with an amused expression. "That's right, I forgot you were the radical in your family. Take after your *padre*, do you? I hear he was involved in some kind of workers' union, *fasci dei lavoratori,* back in the old country."

Luisa looked surprised, but of course I'd already guessed that, although I didn't know the details. Maybe someday Babbo will tell me. I do know this: If he and Mama hadn't been involved in some kind of activism back in Sicily, they never would have let me take part in the strike as much as I did.

Audenzio and I continued to argue. He admitted that what I said about the shirtwaist strike was true. But he thought many of the agreements we'd won with the small shops were weak, and that the big factories, like Triangle, had never really made any concessions.

"Look at poor Rosa, here," he said with a smile. "*Worka worka* all the long day on Saturday!"

Beside me, Luisa was scowling. I knew she didn't approve of all this strike talk, but I couldn't help blurting out, "Well, what about the Italian workers? Will the Italians join in the cloakmakers' strike?"

Audenzio didn't hesitate. "*Sì*, we will. Unlike Local 25, your union, ours has made an effort to involve Italians from the beginning."

In the end, all I could do was wish him luck. I remember how so many shirtwaist workers had to stand on the picket lines in the bitter wind and freezing rain. Maybe striking in the summer will be better. At least it won't be so cold.

Wednesday, June 15, 1910

Sarah has been quiet lately, but now that there's more talk about a cloakmakers' strike, she's beginning to sound like her old self, full of fire and determination. Today at lunch I told her about my conversation with Audenzio. She listened carefully and nodded.

"It's true. We didn't achieve all our goals, like getting closed shops so only union members are hired," she said with a sigh. "And many of the small shops come and go. Since new owners have no agreement with the union, conditions seem to be getting worse again."

"At least we did something to get people excited about labor unions," I argued. I hate to think that all our hard work went for nothing. "And now maybe the cloakmakers can build on what we did."

Sarah knitted her brows, lost in thought. "Yes, but I want to do more. . . ."

"What do you mean?" I asked.

Ever since the strike, Sarah told me, she'd been thinking about becoming a full-time labor organizer. The problem was that her brother, who'd just turned fourteen, wanted to stay in school.

Sarah sighed and picked at a loose thread on her shirt-waist blouse. "Joseph's a smart boy. He might even be able to get a scholarship for college. So I've promised my family to keep working steadily so he can finish high school."

Sarah's brother might be bright, but it's hard to see how anyone could be as smart and determined as Sarah herself. Sometimes I wonder what Sarah could do if only she'd had the chance to stay in school.

Sunday, July 3, 1910

Tonight it was hot, so I dragged out a blanket to use as a bed and slept on the fire escape. My sparrow appeared at dusk, cocking his little head at me. I fed him some bread crumbs. Whenever I see my sparrow, I can't help thinking about Teresa. She was the little bird in our family.

And I wonder how such a tiny creature can survive in this city, when it is so hard for everyone else.

Thursday, July 7, 1910

At lunch today someone in our shop passed a flyer around. It was printed on bloodred paper. It said:

GENERAL STRIKE DECLARED
TODAY 2 P.M.

Today, at 2 p.m. — not earlier, not later — every cloak and skirt worker — operator, tailor, finisher, cutter, presser, buttonhole maker — must put aside his work and together with all other workers go out on strike. Not one of you must remain in the shops! All out!

In the afternoon we heard loud noises from the streets. Out of the corner of my eye I saw a flash of dark hair. Before Mr. Klein could do anything, Sarah jumped up and turned off the power.

"Outside!" she shouted. "We must show support for our fellow workers!"

We piled out, leaving Mr. Klein fuming and grumbling behind us. The street was packed with men and women laughing and shouting. It felt as if every worker in New York City were out on the streets.

Of course, our shop will be back to work as usual in the morning. The shirtwaist workers aren't ready for another strike. But at least on this day, we showed our support for the cloakmakers and their struggle for better conditions.

I hope they can stick together and win. From what Audenzio says, the Italian cloakmakers are standing firm with the Jewish workers. And more Italians have been in-volved in the planning. That's good, I think. I wish it had happened more in our strike. Maybe then things wouldn't have been so hard on our family.

Saturday, July 16, 1910

The cloakmakers' strike is still on. This morning, as we were sitting down at our machines, Sarah leaned over and told me that Rose Schneiderman, that young, red-haired woman I heard give a speech during our strike, is helping negotiate for the women workers.

"That could be you someday, Sarah," I told her. "Why, I think you'd be every bit as good as Rose Schneiderman or Clara Lemlich!"

To my surprise, Sarah flushed with pleasure. "Do you think so, Angela? Do you really think I could do it?"

I assured her that she could. As I sewed, I couldn't help stealing a glance now and then at her sturdy shoulders and dark hair. Sarah always seems so confident about everything. I never guessed she would have doubts about herself. But maybe even strong girls like Sarah need en-couragement sometimes.

As for me, well, translating those speeches into Italian and walking on the picket line a few times was enough.

Sunday, August 7, 1910

With all this talk about the cloakmakers' strike, I've been thinking more and more about last fall. Mostly I wonder what would have happened if the union had waited until the workers were more organized, or if they had made more of an effort to include Italian girls like Luisa, Rosa, and me.

I think about this on Saturday afternoons, waiting for Luisa and Rosa in front of the tall Asch Building on Washington Place. Workers from the Triangle factory were among the first to begin the fight last fall. But how much good did it do them?

Luisa says she likes it fine on the ninth floor, but I wouldn't want to work so high off the ground. And as for Rosa, well, these days it's pretty clear what she likes best — and his name is Audenzio!

Sunday, August 21, 1910

It's hot! Hot, hot, hot! We can't stand to be inside our apartment, day or night. There's not a breath of air. I feel like my skin is sticky all the time with sweat, grime, and dust. And poor Babbo suffers even more than we do. I think I would faint if I had to be a hod carrier in the summer.

This afternoon we sat outside — along with everyone else on Elizabeth Street. The pushcart vendors were selling Italian beans and chickpeas, urging us to buy some to eat while we pass the time.

Zi' Vincenzo, Rosa, Alfio, and Pietro came to sit with us, but soon the little boys were gone, junking with Vito. Vito is quite good at it. He wanders for hours, up and down alleys, looking for things to sell or anything we can use. Rags, old pipes, bottles, wood. Although lately he also seems to have a knack for finding a broken fire hydrant, and cooling off in the water!

Today Zi' Maria leaned out of her window and yelled, "Vito! Bring me back the largest block of ice you can find. I want to sleep on it!"

Even Mama, who hasn't smiled much for months, had to laugh at that.

Still, I'm proud of my brother these days. He's doing well as a shoeshine boy. He has a little cloth bag for his brush, polishes, and cloth. People like him because he has a quick smile and laughing eyes. Who knows? Maybe Vito will become a rich businessman someday like he's always dreamed.

He hasn't said much about missing Teresa, but I know he does, because once I came home to find a piece of *torrone*, almond candy, carefully left on the kitchen table at the place where Teresa always sat.

Later

After our evening meal, we all went back outside. Audenzio came by the apartment just as the sun was setting, sending red streaks into the sky. He settled down to talk about the strike.

"We have hope for a good settlement that will change things from now on," he told Zi' Vincenzo and Babbo. Audenzio sat on one side of Zi' Vincenzo, while Rosa sat on the other.

I caught her eye and smiled. Things are sailing right for her in love these days. I know her papa likes Audenzio, but since Rosa helps so much with Pietro and Alfio, there's no rush for them to marry.

Wednesday, August 24, 1910

Still hot. Sometimes I buy a small piece of ice from the ice wagon for a penny and put it on my face. Then I am cool, even if it only lasts for a few minutes.

Friday, September 2, 1910

Good news: The cloakmakers' strike is over! The agreement was made with all the manufacturers and the union, and was accepted by the workers today. The cloakmakers have won. Everyone is calling the agreement the "Protocol of Peace."

After work, Sarah and I walked to the square near the *Jewish Daily Forward* building on East Broadway to watch the celebration. By seven o'clock the streets were filled. Everyone was hugging and talking. People were so happy.

Audenzio rushed up to us. The Italian workers were streaming in from another union hall, carrying strike leaders on their shoulders. Audenzio was so excited, words tumbled out of him. "We'll get a fifty-hour work week, and double pay for overtime. And ten holidays with pay!"

Audenzio says there is to be a special board to help clean up the dirtiest shops. Most important, they won what we shirtwaist workers did not: union recognition and a closed shop. From now on, employers are to hire only union workers. Only if union workers aren't available can non-union workers be hired. Now the unions are sure to get stronger.

I left early to get home. But the shouts and sounds of

workers celebrating filled my ears for blocks. Maybe life will get better — at least for some of us.

Saturday, September 3, 1910

Sarah and I watched the cloakmakers' parade this afternoon. It was so exciting, with music and flags, and people singing and celebrating. It's a good feeling to think that our strike helped make this one successful. This is important, because this time the large manufacturers have signed, too. But, of course, it doesn't change anything for shirt-waist workers, or in big factories like the Triangle shop.

Still, I had to smile when I heard someone on the street singing:

> *Here's how a tailor sews*
> *He sews like this!*
> *A tailor sews and sews and sews*
> *And he owns nothing, not even his bread!*
> *Once upon a time I could not believe*
> *That we should work from eight to eight!*
> *But now with the strikes*
> *We have no more to work from eight to eight.*

Monday, November 7, 1910

I can't believe how time has gone by. Since the excitement of the cloakmakers' strike is over, everything is back to normal. Mostly I've been too tired to write in my book. Besides, I like sitting outside on my fire escape to write, and the weather is too cold for that now.

Sarah is restless these days. Last week she told me she's decided to go to night school. She squared her shoulders like she used to do and announced in a firm voice, "I don't want to be a shirtwaist worker all my life, Angela."

Sarah is beginning to move on and change, and make something better of her life. But what about me? I'm fifteen now. I've been a shirtwaist worker for more than a year. Will I be one all my life?

Even if Mama didn't need me home at night, I don't know if I could go to night school. When I come home from a long day bent over my sewing machine, my head feels numb and stupid. I just want to sleep.

Instead, I cook and clean and help Mama and Zi' Maria make flowers. Lately, whenever she has the chance, Luisa slips away upstairs to Rosa's apartment. Oh, I know she helps with the boys a lot. But in my heart I know she'd much rather be with Rosa than have anything to do with me.

Wednesday, November 16, 1910

I saw Arturo at his papa's bakery shop today. He asked me how our family was doing without Teresa. What could I tell him? I only shrugged.

Whenever I see Arturo and feel the warmth of his smile, I feel like staring down at my shoes. I can't think of anything to say to him.

Sunday, November 20, 1910

I wonder if Miss Kelly is still teaching school. These days, I just don't know what good practicing my English will do, anyway. I'll probably just keeping working in the factory.

The last time I saw Clara, she looked pale and worn out. I have been getting more colds and coughs myself this fall. When I look ahead, all I can see are long, long days of work.

Thursday, December 8, 1910

Sarah told me that Clara's mother has been talking to a matchmaker and that Clara may become engaged soon. The man is a grocer, and that is a good thing. Clara will be able to work beside her husband in their own business.

I wonder if Sarah will get married. Somehow, I don't think so. Sarah has other dreams. I'm sure she'll reach her goal of becoming a labor organizer. I can just see her making speeches all across the country.

Now that Sarah is back at evening school, she always reads during lunch and doesn't have much time to talk.

The other day, though, Sarah asked me what I dreamed of doing. I shrugged. I wish I knew what I want to do. Luisa and Rosa, I know, dream of getting married and having children of their own. I'd like that someday. It's just that, ever since Teresa died, it's hard to think of the future. Mostly I just get up and go to work, day after day. Most days, I'm too tired to dream.

Monday, February 13, 1911

It's been weeks and weeks since I've written. Babbo has hurt his shoulder again, and hasn't been working. So every night I rush home from work to help Mama, Zi' Maria, and a few other neighbors make artificial flowers.

Not only that, Alfio and Pietro depend on my help with their schoolwork. I'm surprised I still remember my numbers and my English. There's really no one else to help them. Vito is usually working late — not that he would ever remember much about arithmetic. And of course

Rosa and Luisa can't help, because they never went to school in America.

I like helping the boys. But sometimes I feel sad that I never even finished eighth grade.

Thursday, February 16, 1911

Everything seems so dark, grimy, and cold. It is almost a year since Teresa died. Mama doesn't cry as much. But there's still a wall between Luisa and me, a wall that will not come down. We sleep in the same bed and eat at the same table, but things aren't the same.

If only spring would come. Then I would have a place of my own to sit and write again. I can't wait to sit on the fire escape and watch for my sparrow.

Wednesday, February 22, 1911

Well, at last I have something good to write about.

Rosa is officially engaged to Audenzio at last! I am so glad for her. Although he seems hardheaded and talks so much, I think in his heart he's devoted to her. It will be a relief to Zi' Vincenzo to have such a bright son-in-law.

It has been such a sad time, now at last there's some happiness.

Sunday, March 19, 1911

Mama had a little dinner today for Rosa and Audenzio. As a special treat we had a chicken, and also macaroni. We laughed together, although once I caught Mama wiping away tears. She was thinking about Teresa, I know. Just as Rosa was thinking of her mama.

Luisa was quiet. I think maybe she's a little jealous of Rosa. Luisa is probably wanting to be married soon herself. But of course she wouldn't tell me that.

Wednesday, March 22, 1911

Teresa has been gone a year. I went to church with Mama and lit a candle. We don't go to church so much here. We are always working, working. But maybe on Sunday mornings Mama and I will start to go.

Friday, March 24, 1911

The weather is getting a little better. It almost feels like spring. I looked for my sparrow this evening, but I didn't see him.

Sarah says I need cheering up. She says we should start walking to Washington Square Park on Saturday afternoons again like we did last year, to meet Clara, Luisa, and Rosa.

So tomorrow we will go.

Saturday, March 25, 1911

I pick up my pen, but my hand is shaking.

It is late, but Mama can't sleep. She wanders around our three dingy rooms, like a mother bird whose nestling has fallen from the tree. Vito sat awkwardly beside me tonight until he fell asleep. He was silent for once.

Mama made me dark, strong coffee, but I cannot get warm. She wanted me to eat, too, but my body shook too much. No matter what I do, the shivering won't stop.

"Sleep, Angela," she crooned a little while ago. "Do not try to write in your book tonight."

But I'm afraid to sleep, afraid to close my eyes. I put my hands over my ears and try to make the screams go away. But I hear them still.

It happened like this. After work, Sarah and I went to the park at Washington Square to wait for Rosa, Luisa, and Clara. As we walked, I told Sarah that Rosa would be married soon, perhaps in May. "Audenzio will be a good husband. My mama is happy. She thinks of Rosa almost like a daughter."

We stayed in the park until Sarah said, "It's about a quarter to five. They should be leaving work soon."

That's when we heard the cry. "Fire!"

People around us began to run. Sarah grabbed my hand and pulled me along. We ran a little way down Washington Place, to the corner of Greene Street.

Around us, people stopped. They looked up and pointed. And then I saw. Smoke! Smoke was pouring from the top of the Asch Building.

"It's at the Triangle," someone yelled. "Fire in the Triangle Waist Company!"

Smoke poured out from the eighth floor.

Just a few minutes later, something dark tumbled from a window. At first my brain was stupid. I thought it was a large bolt or bundle of cloth someone was trying to save by tossing it out. And so I watched the bundle tumble through the air and land on the sidewalk.

While the bundle was falling, everything seemed to become completely still. And then came an awful, awful sound. Thud.

After that, screams pierced the air. I felt a sharp pain clutch my whole body. A wave of fear and horror made my knees collapse. Everyone seemed to understand at the same instant.

It wasn't a bundle at all. It was a girl.

People screamed again. I looked up. There was another girl in the window. Her clothes and hair were smoking, on fire. Suddenly she stepped into the air, her hands waving. Her skirts billowed around her.

Her arms and legs came hurtling down so fast. Just before she hit the ground, everything went still. All my breath drained out. Then came that same terrible thud.

I screamed again and so did Sarah and everyone near us. And we all yelled the same thing. "No, no! Don't jump! Don't jump! Wait for the fire nets!"

The fire engines were clanging, so I knew they were close. From behind us came the sound of galloping hooves. I turned to look. The fire horses had stopped, panting, their sides heaving. The firemen raced to get their hoses ready.

"Get nets! Hurry! Hurry!" we shouted.

When I turned back, there were more bodies on the sidewalk.

All I could think of was Luisa. Luisa, Rosa, Clara. Trapped. Trapped on the ninth floor.

I pulled at Sarah's sleeve. I wanted to scream, but my

voice came out in a hoarse, terrified whisper. "Luisa. Luisa. Rosa, Clara."

I should go find them, I thought stupidly. I started to push through the crowd. But Sarah grabbed my arm hard and held me. "No. Stay back! Angela, you can't go in there."

Tears were streaming down my face, although I didn't know when I had begun to cry. "Why don't they come out the door? Why are they jumping?"

Sarah shook her head helplessly.

A man next to me said, "A girl who came out the other way said some of the doors are locked. Some girls came down the elevator, but now it's not working."

"The door is locked. The door to the ninth floor must be locked," Sarah began to repeat, over and over. "I remember when I worked here, that door was locked. We all had to file out one narrow passage and one door at the end of the day so they could check our pocketbooks."

Sarah took a ragged breath, her voice choking in her throat. "More than two hundred girls work on that floor."

A woman behind me yelled to the people up front, "Do something! Can't you see that girl in the window is going to jump?"

Some people grabbed a horse blanket from a horse standing nearby. Four men held it out. I watched, putting my hand in my mouth and biting it hard to keep from screaming. Maybe she would be all right. Maybe it would work.

But when the girl landed, the blanket simply gave way.

The firemen rushed to put ladders against the building and hold out their fire nets.

I clutched Sarah. Slowly, slowly, I watched one ladder swing up the side of the building. "It's too short," I whispered in horror. "The ladder isn't tall enough to reach even the eighth floor. And look! The water from the hoses won't reach, either."

"The girls keep leaping. The fire is too hot," Sarah said.

"But the nets! Can't the nets help?"

Another girl leaped. Smoke drifted into the air from her clothes and hair.

She seemed to roll in midair. She hit the net squarely in the middle. The net was only about ten feet around. She came down so fast, she bounced out of the net. She hit the hard sidewalk. After that, she did not move.

The next moment two more girls appeared in the window. I could see red flames from the floor below flashing around their faces. They must have seen the other girl fall. Maybe they even heard the thud. But they threw themselves into the air, anyway. They had to, the fire was too fierce. They twined their arms around one another. They were friends — maybe they were from the same village back in Russia or Italy, or maybe they had sat at sewing machines next to one another, hour after hour.

The firemen did their best. They got the net right under them, but it did nothing. The girls broke through the net.

More girls appeared on the ninth floor. They were pushed together in the windows, screaming. And then the window broke loose and bodies flew through the air, burning hair streaming.

And then one more girl appeared on the ninth floor. I was too far away to see her face. But there was something about her. My heart lurched. Rosa.

I shook my head. "No, no. Rosa! It's Rosa!"

Where was Luisa? Was Luisa behind her in that black smoke?

I saw Rosa move. She couldn't hear my screams, she couldn't see me wave and throw my arms up, as if somehow I could stop her, keep her there, until the ladders reached, until the fire was out. Until . . .

"Rosa! No. No! Don't jump!"

I felt my head get light. The next thing I knew, my cheek was on the ground.

Sarah and a policeman helped me up. "It's no wonder you fainted, miss," he said. "This is the worst I ever saw. You best be gettin' home, dearie, this is no place for you."

Sarah's hands were like ice.

I leaned against her and whispered, "Is the fire out? We must go find them."

"Angela, Angela, listen. Rosa is gone. She's gone, she jumped."

"What about Luisa? Where's Luisa?"

Sarah shook her head. "I didn't see her," she said in a dull flat voice. "Or Clara, either."

The crowd was larger now, people pressing against us. Sarah and I tried to make our way closer, but the policemen kept pushing us back. Dark, black smoke poured out of the windows. The water from a fireman's hose streamed down the sidewalk. It was red with blood. On Greene Street someone stretched out a dark, red canvas. The police began to lay bodies on it in a row.

I saw mothers and fathers wailing and fighting to get past the policemen. Someone jostled me and I tripped. When I got up I had lost Sarah. I tried to call for her. I stood, trembling and shaking, I don't know for how long. I didn't want to give up looking for Luisa.

And then at the edge of the crowd I spotted Tina, Arturo's sister. Tina's face was covered with dirt and blood. She was alone. Staring straight ahead, she began walking away.

Maybe she has seen Luisa, I thought. I began to push

146

through the crowd to follow her. I wanted to call out to her, but by the time I broke free of the crowd she was too far ahead.

I followed Tina for blocks, but she was almost running, and my feet seemed to be made of lead. I don't remember anything I saw on the way home, or even how my feet moved. When Tina disappeared into a tenement, I stopped.

Then I realized I was already on Elizabeth Street. On the next block, I stumbled up the stairs of our tenement. *I have to tell Mama now,* I thought stupidly, not knowing what I would say.

I flung open the door. Everything was empty and still. Mama was gone. Vito was gone. Babbo was gone. Where were they? Did they know?

I spotted Luisa's spring hat on the table. She had finally saved enough money for it. Mama was going to add more flowers to it today so Luisa could wear it tomorrow.

Somehow seeing the hat made my knees so weak, I had to drop to the floor. I started to shake hard. I put my hands over my ears. I could still hear the screams.

I huddled on the kitchen floor, and the tears took hold of me again. Great gulping sobs that made my throat hurt. I cried so hard, I began to choke.

After a while I felt a shadow. The door was still open,

but someone was standing there. I turned and looked, brushing my hair from my eyes. I screamed.

"Luisa!"

She held on to the door frame, as if she might fall down, too. She was bloody and dirty and trembling. She smelled like smoke. Her skirt was torn, her white shirtwaist black with soot. She must have fallen. Her face had a bad scrape that was still bleeding.

Luisa stumbled through the door and fell almost on top of me. She was trembling so hard, I could hardly hold on to her. I kissed her face again and again.

"I got out, Angela. I got out in the last elevator. Then I ran and I got lost and fell," she whispered. "I got separated from Rosa. I wandered around and around, asking everyone, waiting. Then somehow I came home."

"Sarah and I saw the fire. We were coming to meet you. I thought you were dead, I thought you were dead." I said it over and over. I grabbed her dark hair, full of ashes, and pulled it. I kept my arm around her neck. But she didn't seem to mind.

She was warm and her heart was beating. I whispered, "I'm sorry, Luisa. I'm sorry."

She held on to my shoulders. "Angela. I lost Rosa. Did you see Rosa?"

I thought I could write everything in this book. But I can't write this.

Sunday, March 26, 1911
Early Morning

I am sitting on the fire escape. But yesterday the fire escape at the factory was useless. It collapsed, and the people on it died.

I pieced together what happened. Luisa had come down the elevator. Somehow she'd gotten out and been swept into the crowd. She was confused and in shock. Eventually she made her way home, just as I had.

Earlier, Zi' Vincenzo had heard about the fire. He went to fetch Mama and Babbo and Vito. Together they set out to look for Rosa and Luisa. When Mama and Babbo and Vito returned home later, exhausted and frightened, Luisa and I were still on the kitchen floor, clutching each other.

Mama took one step and collapsed to the floor with us. Babbo cried, tears rolling down his worn face. It seemed to me we cried for hours, petting Luisa's hair and holding on to her hands. Even Vito cried.

But Luisa does not cry now. Now that she knows Rosa is gone, she blames herself. She is too sad for tears.

I didn't tell Luisa I saw Rosa fall. I told her I knew that Rosa was dead, but I didn't say I saw her jump. I think she knows, but she will never ask.

Sometimes I still want to put my hands over my ears to stop the screams. I think that even if I live to be old, I'll still be able to hear those sounds, smell the smoke, see girls leaping through the air.

If only people could be like birds. If only we had wings.

Later

Zi' Vincenzo and Audenzio went to look for Rosa. They found her in the temporary morgue, a covered pier on the East River, on East 26th Street. There the bodies have been laid out, with numbers on them.

Bless Audenzio. He would not let Zi' Vincenzo go alone to identify his only daughter.

Before Bed

This afternoon, after we had been sitting for a while with Zi' Vincenzo and the boys, I got up and whispered to Luisa, "I must find out about Clara. I must go see Sarah."

Without a word, Luisa got ready to come with me. We held hands as we walked down the street. Every few steps someone stopped Luisa to hug her and cry. It took us a long time to get to Orchard Street.

I remembered where Sarah's tenement was. We walked up the stairs. When Sarah opened the door, Luisa threw herself in Sarah's arms. They hugged for a long time, though they've never been friendly.

Sarah told us that Clara was dead. She had tried to escape on the elevator, the way Luisa had. But the last elevator had gone. Clara had fallen into the elevator shaft. She had fallen on top of a girl who was already dead.

"We tried to get out the door to the stairs on the Washington Place side," Luisa whispered. "The door was locked. I thought Rosa was right behind me. . . ."

We stood together. Sarah's father came over. He put his hand gently on my arm and spoke to me in Yiddish. I think it was a prayer.

Tuesday, March 28, 1911

Last night I sat on the fire escape until it grew dark. Luisa came out to tell me it was time to come in.

Then suddenly she sat down beside me and asked, "Do you remember the story of Teresa and the goat man?"

I shook my head. Luisa began to speak in a low voice, telling me a story from long ago, in our village in Sicily, when we used to get milk in the mornings from a man who had a herd of goats. The families would bring a bottle and gather round, and he would hold the bottle and squeeze the goat's milk right into it.

"One day when Teresa was little — maybe only two — I was watching her for Mama," Luisa said. "We went to get milk from the goat man. Teresa watched the bottle fill up, her eyes as large as the dark center of a sunflower! While I was paying the goat man, she broke free of my hand and went right up to the goat. She patted its nose and said, '*Grazie.*'"

Luisa laughed. "It was a very bad-tempered goat! That goat butted her head right against Teresa and knocked her into the dirt! Teresa burst into tears. After that she wouldn't drink goat's milk for a week."

Luisa began to cry. She turned her face to look up at the sky. I looked up, too. But it was too cloudy to see any stars. I reached over and squeezed Luisa's hand. She squeezed mine back.

Wednesday, March 29, 1911

People walk around stupidly. For a minute you forget, then the shadow falls back on you again.

One hundred and forty-six people died.

It doesn't seem possible that I am still working every day, as if nothing has changed. But what can we do? We must work to eat and eat to live.

Sarah is still strong. Her resolve to fight for justice is greater than ever. Today she read me part of a poem from the *Jewish Daily Forward*, by a man named Morris Rosenfeld. I don't remember all the words, but I remember one part:

> *Sisters mine, oh my sisters; brethren*
> *Hear my sorrow:*
> *See where the dead are hidden in dark corners,*
> *Where life is choked from those who labor...*

> *Over whom shall we weep first?*
> *Over the burned ones?*
> *Over those beyond recognition?*
> *Over those who have been crippled?*
> *Or driven senseless?*
> *Or smashed?*
> *I weep for them all.*

Thursday, March 30, 1911

Every day there is a funeral. Rosa's was today. Her hearse was white. As the procession passed down the street, the people at the pushcarts stopped. Some of the men took off their hats and bowed their heads.

The church was full to bursting, and Zi' Vincenzo had to be held upright, he was so weak with tears. He has lost so much. Pietro sat silently, but Alfio kept his head buried in Mama's lap.

There is a Red Cross committee to give relief. They agreed to pay for Rosa's funeral and a headstone. Babbo said the cost was about one hundred dollars.

Later

Vito showed me a notice today that read, " 'The Triangle Waist Company begs to notify their customers that they are in good working order. Headquarters now on University Place.' "

Friday, March 31, 1911

Some girls are unclaimed, their bodies left in the morgue. No one knows who they are. Sarah says one girl was identified by a braid in her hair, another by a darn in her sock, another by her engagement ring. But no one has come for these.

Perhaps they were truly alone here, without family, living as boarders in some house or with a family so poor, they were not noticed.

There are seven without names.

Saturday, April 1, 1911

Late last night I heard Babbo talking about returning to Sicily. But Mama surprised me with her answer. She said no. She said Teresa is buried here and she won't leave her.

Luisa has not gone out since Rosa's funeral. Somehow that made it worse for her. She sits and stares. Luisa feels it is her fault. She thought Rosa was right there, right beside her. But, instead, Rosa got pushed into the panic of girls close to the windows.

I know this much: Luisa will not go back to work at the Triangle factory.

I went to the market to get salt, sardines, and bread for Mama. Arturo was at the bakery. He asked about Luisa and gave me a free loaf of bread. His sister Tina is safe, but even Arturo is not smiling these days.

Later

Audenzio came to visit us this evening, and Mama gave him some coffee. She's grateful that Audenzio went with

Zi' Vincenzo to the morgue. It would have been too much for Zi' Vincenzo to go alone to see those pine coffins lined up, one beside the other in a row.

Now I wonder what Zi' Vincenzo will do. Perhaps he will go back home to Sicily. For it will be hard to work and take care of two little boys here, even with Zi' Maria and Mama and other *paesani* to help.

I have not seen my sparrow friend for a long time. I wonder if he has a nest someplace and is too busy to visit me. Or maybe he has flown away from here. Sometimes that is what I want to do, too.

Sunday, April 2, 1911

Sarah had told me there was to be a large memorial meeting at the big Metropolitan Opera House today at three o'clock. I thought for a long time.

This morning while Babbo was drinking coffee I got up my courage. I told him I wanted to go to a memorial meeting for Rosa and the other people who had died.

I did not know what Babbo would say, or what I would do if he said no. But Babbo looked up at me, then nodded. "Okay," he answered me in English. "Okay you go."

•　　•　　•

Sarah was waiting for me near the steps of the Opera House. Streaming in the doors beside us were gentlemen in high black hats and ladies in furs and hats with beautiful long feathers. They sat in the opera boxes while Sarah and I scurried to seats in the balcony.

"There are so many fine-looking ladies and gentlemen here, Sarah," I whispered.

But Sarah shrugged. Her words sounded bitter. "No doubt they are very pleased with themselves for opening their pocketbooks for the families of the poor dead girls."

What did Sarah mean? Wasn't it a good thing that these rich ladies and men wanted to help? But I was afraid to ask her more. Sarah's eyes have seemed angrier than ever since the fire. I wonder if she blames herself for Clara's death. But what could she have done?

Then the speeches began. The first announcement brought loud cheers. The relief committee had received a total of seventy-five thousand dollars to help the families of the Triangle workers. No matter what Sarah said, I was glad that these people were willing to help people like Zi' Vincenzo.

Then some of the speakers began to call for the formation of committees to look into fire protection. Around us, workers began to hiss and jeer. A man in front of me yelled, "You never cared about that before you had to watch girls jump to the sidewalk!"

I shivered. Sarah gripped my arm and pointed. "Look, Rose Schneiderman is getting up to speak."

I remembered Rose, with her fiery red hair. She had inspired the girls in our strike. She had worked in the cloakmakers' strike, too. She looked tiny on the stage. The great hall suddenly became absolutely still. I leaned forward on the edge of my seat.

Rose Schneiderman's speech was not long. I don't remember all she said. But I will never forget these words:

> The life of men and women is so cheap and property is so sacred! There are so many of us for one job, it matters little if 140-odd are burned to death. . . . But every time the workers come out in the only way they know to protest against conditions which are unbearable, the strong hand of the law is allowed to press down heavily upon us.
>
> I can't talk fellowship to you who are gathered here. Too much blood has been spilled. I know from experience it is up to the working people to save themselves. And the only way is through a strong working-class movement.

Suddenly I understood, the way you wipe a window clear of mist.

We must save ourselves. That is what our strike was about. But the strike was just the beginning.

We must keep fighting.

Monday, April 3, 1911

This weekend, flyers were distributed everywhere. There will be a funeral parade on Wednesday at one in the afternoon for the seven dead who have been unclaimed. The mayor has said that their bodies can be buried in Evergreen Cemetery in Brooklyn.

The flyers were written in English, Yiddish, and Italian. I took one in English and read it to Mama, Babbo, Luisa, and Vito as we ate our macaroni tonight.

The flyer said that all workers are called upon to make "a last sad tribute of sympathy and affection."

I took a breath. "Babbo, I would like to leave work on Wednesday to march in the parade."

Babbo looked into my eyes and nodded slowly. Then he cleared his throat and looked around the table at each of us. "That is right, Angela. And I will come to watch. You, too, Mama, you come, with Vito. And you, Luisa. It is time you went outside again."

Babbo stood up and headed toward the door. He put his hand on the doorknob. "Angela is a smart girl, Mama. No?"

Mama nodded. "*Sì*, she did well in school. She has almost filled up that little book her teacher gave her, all in English. Perhaps she would like to go to night school, as some girls do."

Then, to my surprise, Luisa cleared her throat and spoke up. "Angela is a good worker, too. She is respected as a girl who stands up for her beliefs and is willing to fight for others."

Luisa looked directly at me. "Sometimes people say to me, 'Aren't you Angela Denoto's sister? I heard her translate speeches during the shirtwaist strike. That young girl has courage.'"

Luisa paused, her eyes glistening with tears. "And I tell them, '*Sì*, Angela is my sister, and I'm proud of her.'"

I have almost reached the end of my book. Tonight I looked back and read my scratchy handwriting and my simple words. I thought about all that has changed since Miss Kelly gave me this diary.

Perhaps next week I will visit Miss Kelly at school and show her my book. I have a question to ask her, too. I would like to know more about evening school.

160

Miss Kelly said that if I filled the pages, she would give me a new book. Instead, though, I will buy a new one for myself with money I have saved. Maybe I'll even buy two. One, I will keep. The other I will give to Miss Kelly to pay her back for this one. She can give it to the next Italian girl who leaves school.

Yes, that is what I will do.

Tuesday, April 4, 1911

Sarah stood up at the end of the day, just as the machines were shut off and a hush came into the room. She announced in a loud voice that tomorrow there would be a parade of workers to bury the unclaimed dead. She looked at Mr. Klein. "We will all go tomorrow afternoon," she said.

Mr. Klein stood still a moment. He nodded and cleared his throat. It was as if he knew it would be useless to resist. And so he announced, "This shop is closed tomorrow afternoon."

Zi' Vincenzo came to eat macaroni with us tonight, along with Pietro and Alfio. He says a Red Cross lady has been to visit him. The Red Cross will give him money because Rosa died in the fire.

Zi' Vincenzo has decided to go back to Sicily. Perhaps he will come back soon with a new wife.

But later, when Zi' Maria heard this, her eyes twinkled. "Let him go home for a visit. But I don't think he needs to look so far as Sicily to find a new wife. When the time comes . . ."

Well, at that I had to smile. My guess is that Zi' Vincenzo will come back to Elizabeth Street alone. After all, who can dare go against what Zi' Maria wants?

It was also decided that the boys will stay here with us while their father visits Sicily.

"That's good," said Vito. "My shoeshine business is doing so well, I can use Pietro's help as my assistant."

I think we're all glad about this. We've lost so much, but having Pietro and Alfio here will make our hearts lighter.

Wednesday, April 5, 1911

It was dark and wet this morning, almost as if the skies had decided to cry. All the girls left work together and met the parade at Seward Park, near East Broadway and Canal Street. At one o'clock an empty hearse covered with flowers and pulled by six white horses passed by.

I didn't have a hat, and the rain streamed on top of my

head and into my eyes. No one spoke. As one, we began to follow behind the hearse. Along the way, in the tenements, women leaned out their windows and waved white handkerchiefs. They were silent at first. But as we passed, low mourning moans burst from their lips.

As we passed, the windows emptied and the doors of the tenements opened. The women and men and children who had been watching came out and joined the procession, until it swelled larger and larger.

All the while it rained on us. The mud soaked my thin shoes, but I marched through the puddles just the same.

We got to Washington Square, and the park was filled with people. From the park we could see the Asch Building, where the Triangle factory was. Suddenly there was a loud piercing wail. We held hands without caring whose hand we gripped.

We were supposed to march by the building. But the policemen were afraid of a riot, so the line moved under the arch in Washington Square and up Fifth Avenue. We formed lines of eight across. I don't know how many people marched today. I heard a policeman say more than one hundred thousand, with thousands more lined up to watch.

Sometimes in the crowds of people here, I feel invisible. If I disappeared, no one would miss me. But today it felt good to be with other people. I didn't feel alone. I felt part of something. And, somehow, I didn't feel so hopeless.

We held hands and our bodies bumped against one another and we walked in step in the rain. And I thought that if only we could keep walking together, maybe we could change something.

We marched until night came. Once, I tripped, and Sarah put out her hand to steady me. Her hand on my arm felt firm and alive. That made me cry, thinking how Rosa and Clara and all the others would never taste rain again, or feel the warm touch of someone's hand, or see the lamps glowing yellow in the night.

The rain never stopped. At first I wiped cold drops off my face. After a while I didn't bother. I didn't want to let go of the hands I clutched. And so the cold rain mixed with my tears and streamed down my face.

Then from one of the tall towers around us a bell began to ring. It was a deep, sad chime. It seemed to echo through the whole of New York City.

I suppose it was just a clock.

But to me it seemed as if the bell were listening — that somehow the bell could hear our sorrow.

And so it was crying, just as we were, for all the girls who had died.

Epilogue

Angela did return to her old school to show her diary to Miss Kelly. Through the years, she continued to keep a diary and often donated blank journals to elementary schools as gifts for students. Although some children probably used them for scribbling, or even for toilet paper, that didn't bother Angela. She simply wanted to encourage others to write about their lives.

In 1912, Sarah Goldstein left factory work to become an organizer and speaker for the International Ladies' Garment Workers' Union. She traveled all over the country and often wrote newspaper and magazine articles. Sarah never married, but she was a devoted aunt to her brother's four children. Sarah and Angela remained friends throughout their lives.

In 1912, during the strikes of textile workers in Lawrence, Massachusetts, organized by the Industrial Workers of the World, some Italian children were sent to families in New York City to be cared for while their parents were on strike. Through their network of contacts and friends, the Denoto family became involved and took in two children.

During this time, Audenzio continued to visit the

Denoto family. At first, Angela suspected he liked Luisa. When she mentioned this to Luisa, her sister laughed. It was clear to everyone else that Audenzio's real interest was Angela herself. With the blessing of their families and friends, Angela and Audenzio married in 1915, when she was twenty.

Audenzio became a union organizer. The couple's home was a center for labor meetings and discussions. Audenzio and Angela had three daughters: Teresa, Rosie, and Claire. All finished high school. It gave Angela deep satisfaction to see her daughter Teresa graduate from college and go on to receive a master's degree in social work with a special interest in children and public health.

When Angela was seventy-three, her daughters helped her self-publish a memoir of her experiences during the shirtwaist strike and the Triangle fire, based on the diary she kept as a teenager. In 1971, sixty years after the Triangle fire, Angela attended several commemoration events. At these events Angela often read a portion of her eyewitness account of the tragedy.

Angela survived her husband and lived long enough to see her namesake and granddaughter, Angela, earn a doctorate in sociology at New York University. The university now owns the Asch Building, where the Triangle Waist Company fire occurred.

Luisa married a grocer from Elizabeth Street, from a family her parents knew well. She and her husband moved to New Jersey, where they raised their two children. Angela's father was killed in a construction accident ten years after the Triangle fire, and Angela's mother went to live with Luisa for the rest of her days.

Vito started a restaurant supply business and became very successful. Two of his best workers were Alfio and Pietro, who rose through the ranks to become managers. The boys' success pleased their father, Vincenzo, as well as their stepmother, Maria.

Life in America
in 1909

HISTORICAL NOTE

The Shirtwaist Strikes and the Triangle Fire

Hear My Sorrow takes place at one of the most vibrant and tumultuous times in American history, when millions of immigrants came to these shores seeking jobs, education, and better lives. Some fled poverty in their homelands, while others fled political and religious oppression. Many of these immigrants settled in New York City, where they found jobs in the growing ready-to-wear garment industry.

Most workers in the garment industry were young Jewish and Italian immigrants living on New York City's Lower East Side. By 1910, women made up 70 percent of the approximately 83,000 workers in the garment industry. There were more than 2,700 factories, many of them small shops called sweatshops. About 600 shops, employing about 35,000 to 40,000 workers, mostly teenagers and young women, made shirtwaist blouses, a popular style at the time.

Conditions in the shops were harsh, and pay was low. Workers were often employed not by owners, but by subcontractors, who purchased material from a textile manufacturer and hired workers to cut and sew the garments. These subcontractors passed on as many costs as possible to their workers. Women machine operators generally earned anywhere from $7 to $14 a week. Learners usually began at $3 to $4 a week. Often these young women worked fifty-six hours a week or more.

The shirtwaist strike of 1909–1910, often called the "Uprising of the Twenty Thousand," is one of the most important strikes in United States history. It was the largest strike of women that had ever taken place up to that point, and it demonstrated that women could be a force in America's labor movement.

The shirtwaist strike brought women of various social classes together in a common effort to seek justice. The strike was led by the International Ladies' Garment Workers' Union (ILGWU), founded in 1900. The New York City group, Local 25, came into being a few years later, in 1906. The union was young and small, with less than a thousand members before the strike began in 1909. One of the most fascinating aspects of the strike was the involvement of middle- and upper-class women in the Women's Trade Union League (WTUL), led by Mary Dreier, who helped bring the struggle to the attention of the public.

In the fall of 1909, small strikes had been taking place

against shops such as the Triangle Waist Company. On November 22, 1909, at a meeting in the "Great Hall" at Cooper Union, a machine operator named Clara Lemlich called for a general strike of all workers.

As the strike progressed, the public was surprised at the solidarity the young, inexperienced immigrant women showed. Union leaders guessed that a few thousand Jewish workers would heed the call to strike, but by the end of the day on Wednesday, November 23, about 20,000 workers had walked off the job. Shop owners hired thugs and prostitutes to intimidate, hassle, and even beat the girls. Police officers were bribed. Hundreds of strikers were arrested.

New research has helped bring to light the complex nature of this strike. Until recently, most of the research and writing on the shirtwaist strike dismissed the role of the Italian women in the strike, concluding that they simply were not involved, or were apathetic. (Of the 15,000 to 25,000 young women who went out on strike, most were Jewish immigrants, whereas only about 2,000 were Italian immigrants.)

Contemporary scholars, relying on Italian-language newspapers, oral histories, and other sources, are helping shed new light on the complex relationship of Italian women and their families during the 1909 strike. This new research points to a history of activism back in Italy by parents of the girls involved in the strike, as well as to a distrust of American unions such as the ILGWU in favor of more militant organizations such as the Industrial Workers of the World. After the shirtwaist strikes, Italian-American women became an integral part of the U.S. labor movement, playing leading roles in many subsequent strikes. In this book I have tried to suggest the complexity of these issues, as well as the tension in one Italian family as its members try to balance a commitment to social activism with the struggle for day-to-day existence.

Striking during the cold winter weather of 1909–1910 was a hardship for the young women and their families. Since the union was small, it didn't have a large strike fund set aside. The smaller shops were more likely to settle with the union quickly because they could not afford a work stoppage. But the larger companies formed a group called the Association of Waist and Dress Manufacturers of New York and vowed to hold out against a settlement.

As strike funds became scarce and more and more of the smaller shops settled, enthusiasm for the strike began to dwindle. In mid-February 1910, the strike ended. By then, the union had signed agreements with nearly 340 shops. But the agreements with about thirteen of the larger manufacturers were compromises. One of these shops was the Triangle Waist Company, which had kept its doors open throughout the strike. In the end, Triangle did not accede to all the union's demands, including the demand for a closed shop — that is, to hire only union workers. Conditions at shops like Triangle did not really improve.

The Triangle Waist Company was located on the eighth, ninth, and tenth floors of the ten-story Asch Building in lower Manhattan. On Saturday, March 25, 1911, at approximately 4:45 p.m., a fire started on the eighth floor. The bell to end work had just started ringing. In another few minutes, the workers would have been gone.

The fire began on the eighth floor and spread rapidly. Within minutes the heat and smoke became unbearable, and the fire soon spread to the ninth floor. In the ensuing panic, girls found that the door to the stairs on the Washington Place side of the building was locked. Some girls were pushed to the windows by the heat and flames, and from there they jumped. The firemen's ladders reached only the sixth floor. The nets did nothing to break their falls.

The Asch Building was supposedly "fireproof," but it had no sprinklers. Its one inadequate fire escape collapsed under the heat and the weight of the people on it, throwing workers to their deaths. The Triangle fire was brought under control in less than a half hour. Ironically, the building itself didn't suffer much structural damage. But 146 workers, mostly young women and girls, died.

New Yorkers were shocked by the tragedy. On April 2, at a memorial meeting at the Metropolitan Opera House, labor organizer Rose Schneiderman made an impassioned speech castigating citizens and public officials who had not supported the workers' strike in 1909. Giving money in the aftermath of the tragedy was not enough, she insisted.

In the aftermath of the Triangle fire, the Factory Investigating Commission, headed by Robert Wagner and Al Smith (who later became governor of New York), was formed to investigate conditions in factories. Eventually the state of New York passed extensive reform laws that began to address the need for safety standards in the workplace.

Despite pouring rain, more than 120,000 people participated in a memorial march on April 5, 1911, in honor of seven unidentified victims of the fire. Isaac Harris and Max Blanck, owners of the Triangle Waist Company, were investigated and brought to trial for manslaughter, but found not guilty.

The Lower East Side was characterized by lines of laundry hanging between buildings, crossing courtyards and air shafts.

The bustling streets of the Lower East Side were filled with pushcarts, peddlers, and people shopping and socializing.

175

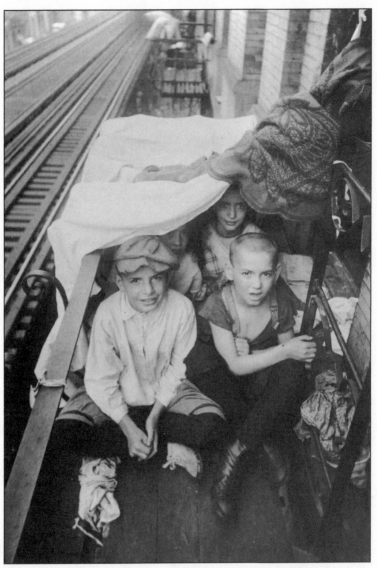

Children play on a tenement fire escape, which could serve as an extension of the apartment, or a refuge from sweltering heat in the summers.

An Italian family works making artificial flowers in a dim tenement apartment, lit only by a gas lamp. Laundry and rags hang above them.

In the sweatshops of the New York City garment industry, conditions were terrible for workers. Doors and windows were frequently locked, and the workers were almost always underpaid and forced to work long hours.

Women march to New York's City Hall during the long, difficult weeks of the shirtwaist strike. There were many cases in which the strikers were beaten or arrested by police officers and abused by company goons or other workers.

Firefighters work to extinguish the fire smoldering within the Triangle Waist Company. However, they encountered disastrous difficulties. Their hoses were unable to reach the top floors of the building, and the nets were too weak to support the girls jumping to escape the fire.

In the aftermath of the Triangle Waist Company fire, mourners came together to honor the victims and pay their respects to the unidentified dead. The 400,000 who turned up marched silently in the rain, and vowed to see justice in the campaign for worker protection.

The Uprising of the Twenty Thousand

Dedicated to the Waistmakers of 1909

In the black of the winter of nineteen nine,
When we froze and bled on the picket line,
We showed the world that women could fight
And we rose and won with women's might.

Chorus:

Hail the waistmakers of nineteen nine,
Making their stand on the picket line,
Breaking the power of those who reign,
Pointing the way, smashing the chain.

And we gave new courage to the men
Who carried on in nineteen ten
And shoulder to shoulder we'll win through,
Led by the I.L.G.W.U.

Labor union song about the 1909 shirtwaist strike.

GLOSSARY

Italians came to America from many parts of Italy, where they often spoke different dialects. In New York City, a kind of pidgin (called Itaglish) developed in the marketplace.

Italian or Sicilian Dialect

Babbo: Daddy, familiar term for "Father"
Buon giorno: good morning
cortile: courtyard
fasci dei lavoratori: workers' unions
grazie: thank you
grignollo/a: greenhorn, newcomer
mio padre: my father
onore di famiglia: family honor
paesani: neighbors, people from the same town
salotto: parlor, front room
sarta: seamstress or tailoress
sì: yes
soggiorno: dining and living area in Sicilian household
torrone: almond candy
turnialettu: bed flounce
Zi': Sicilian familiar dialect for "uncle" (zio) or "aunt" (zia)
zuppa: soup

Itaglish (American Loan Words)

boifrendo: boyfriend
bosso: boss
operatrici: sewing machine operators
scioppa: shop
worka: work

Yiddish Words

pogrom: raids and massacres
shetl: Jewish town
sheitel: wig

ABOUT THE AUTHOR

About the writing of *Hear My Sorrow*, Deborah Hopkinson says, "Before I began this book, I knew very little about the 1909 shirtwaist strikes and the Triangle Waist Company fire. To research the story, I consulted many books and articles, poured over library photo collections, listened to oral history tapes, visited the Lower East Side Tenement Museum, and wandered through the neighborhoods where Angela and her family would have lived.

"The story seemed to really come alive at the moment I stood on the sidewalk outside the building that once housed the Triangle Waist Company, and imagined myself there on that March afternoon so long ago.

"It has been a privilege, and a responsibility, to write about these brave young women. Most of their fellow citizens didn't see these young immigrant workers as individual human beings, with hopes and dreams. It took a tragedy, and the ceaseless efforts of workers, labor organizers, and reformers, to help bring about real improvements in factories.

"While we now have laws to protect workers, tragedies

can still happen if laws are not enforced. On September 3, 1991, twenty-five people, mostly women, died in the Imperial Food Products chicken-processing plant in Hamlet, North Carolina. Another fifty-three people were injured, and forty-nine children were orphaned in the disaster. Some of the workers who tried to escape couldn't get out, because the exits had been locked or blocked to prevent people from stealing. Although there were laws, the plant had never had an official state inspection in its eleven years. Following the fire, North Carolina passed new laws for worker safety. The plant was torn down in 2001 to make way for a memorial park."

Deborah Hopkinson is the author of such award-winning children's books as *Sweet Clara and the Freedom Quilt; Girl Wonder, A Baseball Story in Nine Innings;* and *A Band of Angels.* Her nonfiction book, *Shutting Out the Sky: Life in the Tenements of New York 1880–1924,* also chronicles this period of New York's history. It was selected as one of the New York Public Library's 100 Books for Reading and Sharing, an ALA Notable Trade Book in Social Studies, and it was awarded an Orbis Pictus Honor and a Jane Addams Honor.

ACKNOWLEDGMENTS

Writing *Hear My Sorrow* has been a deeply rewarding experience. I have learned so much, and wish to thank the many people who helped make this book possible. Throughout this project I was fortunate to meet Amy Griffin, Lisa Sandell, and Beth Levine, three amazing and talented editors. I am especially grateful to Lisa for her encouragement and thoughtfulness, and to Amy for her enthusiasm and unflagging support. Thanks also to Steven Malk, my agent, for setting me on the path that led into this fascinating period of history.

I feel fortunate to have had the advice of two scholars whose writings and research have been extraordinarily helpful. Donna R. Gabaccia, Charles H. Stone Professor of American History at the University of North Carolina at Charlotte, was thorough and generous in reviewing the manuscript, and her book on social change among Italian immigrants on the Lower East Side was invaluable. Dr. Gabaccia introduced me to Dr. Jennifer Guglielmo, Assistant Professor of History at Smith College, whose research enabled me to better understand Italian labor history during this period, and who also gave generously of her time to read the manuscript and respond to queries. Any errors are my own.

A special thanks goes to author Susan Campbell Bartoletti, whose advice during one long phone call was more helpful than she probably ever imagined, and whose work I deeply admire. I would also like to thank the staff members who assisted me with research at libraries and museums, especially Patrizio Sizione and Barbara Morley at Cornell University's Kheel Center for Labor-Management Documentation and Archives, and the library staff of the Museum of the City of New York, the New York Public Library, the Library of Congress, the New-York Historical Society, and New York University.

Mahalo to my dear friend Elisa Johnston, her daughter Kate, and late mother Laurie Johnston, for welcoming me into their family home on Jones Street in Greenwich Village. I will always remember our visit to the Lower East Side Tenement Museum. My husband, Andy Thomas, and my children, Rebekah and Dimitri, who bring me joy every day. I am fortunate to have many people whose friendship and support sustains me day to day. A special thanks to my sisters, Janice Fairbrother and Bonnie Johnson, my friends, especially Michele Hill, Vicki Hemphill, Deborah Wiles, and Jane Kurtz, and all of my Whitman College colleagues.

Grateful acknowledgment is made for permission to reprint the following:

Morris Rosenfeld's poem in honor of the Triangle fire victims, which is excerpted on page 153 of this book, was first published in the *Jewish Daily Forward* on March 29, 1909. It has been reprinted and translated in *The Triangle Fire* by Leon Stein (New York: Carroll & Graf, 1962), pages 145–146.

Rose Schneiderman's speech at the Metropolitan Opera House on April 2, 1911, which is excerpted on page 158 of this book, was first published in *The Survey*, April 8, 1911. It is quoted in *Out of the Sweatshop: The Struggle for Industrial Democracy* by Leon Stein, editor, (New York: Quadrangle/New Times Book Company, 1977), pages 196–197.

Cover portrait: Detail from Paul Hoffman Jr. High School, Photo by S. Gardner, Museum of the City of New York, Gift of Mrs. William G. Hassler, Negative no. 01.35.1.255.

Cover background: Culver Pictures, New York.

Page 176, top: Tenement clotheslines, Collections of the Library of Congress, No. LC-D4-36490.

Page 176, bottom: Lower East Side market, Collection of the New-York Historical Society, Negative no. 71078.

Page 177: Children on fire escape, Museum of the City of New York, Gift of Tenement House Department, New York City, Negative no. 31.93.14.

Page 178, top: Family making artificial flowers, Getty Images, New York.

Page 178, bottom: Garment factory, Underwood Picture Archives/Super Stock, New York.

Page 179, top: Women picketers, Library of Congress, No. LC-USZ62-49516.

Page 179, bottom: Picketers marching to City Hall, UNITE Archives Kheel Center, Cornell University, Ithaca, New York.

Page 180: Triangle factory fire, Getty Images, New York.

Page 181, top: Triangle fire memorial parade, UNITE Archives Kheel Center, Cornell University, Ithaca, New York.

Page 181, bottom: Memorial parade in the rain, UNITE Archives Kheel Center, Cornell University, Ithaca, New York.

Page 182: "The Uprising of the Twenty Thousand" song from *Let's Sing!* Educational Department, International Ladies' Garment Workers' Union, New York, New York, n.d.

OTHER DEAR AMERICA
AND MY NAME IS AMERICA BOOKS
ABOUT NEW YORK CITY

My Name Is America: The Journal of Finn Reardon
A Newsie
By Susan Campbell Bartoletti

Dear America: One Eye Laughing, The Other Weeping
The Diary of Julie Weiss
By Barry Denenberg

Dear America: Dreams in the Golden Country
The Diary of Zipporah Feldman, a Jewish Immigrant Girl
By Kathryn Lasky

Dear America: When Christmas Comes Again
The World War I Diary of Simone Spencer
By Beth Seidel Levine

With love and gratitude to Robert Aitken
and in memory of Anne Aitken.
Thank you for your dedication
to peace and social justice,
and for showing the way.

While the events described and some of the characters in this book may be based on
actual historical events and real people, Angela Denoto is a fictional character, created by
the author, and her journal and the epilogue are works of fiction.

Copyright © 2004 by Deborah Hopkinson

All rights reserved. Published by Scholastic Inc.
DEAR AMERICA®, SCHOLASTIC, and associated logos are trademarks
and/or registered trademarks of Scholastic Inc.

Library of Congress Cataloging-in-Publication Data
Hopkinson, Deborah.
Hear my sorrow: the diary of Angela Denoto, a shirtwaist worker / by Deborah Hopkinson
p. cm. — (Dear America)
ISBN 0-439-22161-7
Summary: Forced to drop out of school at the age of fourteen to help support her family,
Angela, an Italian immigrant, works long hours for low wages in a garment factory, and becomes
a participant in the shirtwaist worker strikes of 1909.
[1. Factories — Fiction.   2. Labor disputes — Fiction.   3. Immigrants — Fiction.   4. Italian
Americans — Fiction.   5. Diaries — Fiction.   6. New York (N.Y.) — History —
1898–1951 — Fiction.]   I. Title.   II. Series.
PZ7.H778125 He 2004
[Fic] 22   2003021454
CIP AC
10 9 8 7 6 5 4 3 2 1   04 05 06 07 08 09

The display type was set in PanAm Regular.
The text type was set in Centaur.
Book design by Steve Hughes
Photo research by Amla Sanghvi

Printed in the U.S.A.
First edition, October 2004